Homicide: Saigon

Stephen Mertz

WOLFPACK PUBLISHING
— EST 2013 —

WOLFPACK
PUBLISHING
— EST 2013 —

The characters and events portrayed in this book are fic-
titious. Any similarity to real persons, living or dead, is
coincidental and not intended by the author.

Text copyright © 2021 Stephen Mertz

Published by Wolfpack Publishing
5130 S. Fort Apache Road, 215-380
Las Vegas, NV 89148

Paperback IBSN 978-1-64734-716-1
eBook ISBN 978-1-64734-715-4

Homicide: Saigon

This one is for
Bill Fieldhouse

Praise for Stephen Mertz

....

"One of the best writers in the genre!" —Max Allan Collins

"The cleanest, strongest prose in the business!" —Gravetapping.com

"Stephen Mertz writes a hard-edged, fast-paced thriller for those who like their tales straight and sharp!" —Joe R. Lansdale

"One of the best adventure writers of our time!" —James M. Reasoner

Table of Contents

....

HOMICIDE: SAIGON

Chapter 1

....

South Vietnam. 1970

Cord McGavin crouched in deep shadow behind a rotted wooden post at the foot of the pier.

Heat rose from the filthy waters of the Saigon. The temperature and the humidity were in the upper 90s. The night reeked of algae, garbage, dead fish and fuel oil. Even now, an hour past midnight, the broad, muddy river was busy with the hooting and tooting of tug boats and passing ships from the sea some miles away. Moonlight dappled the swells of the passing ships, while sampans and flat, high-stern, evil-smelling junks bobbed on the wide expanse of water.

The hubbub of Lam Son Square, near the center of downtown Saigon, could have been a million miles away, not the walking distance that had brought McGavin here.

He was an investigator, assigned to a special operations unit of the US Army's Joint Criminal Investigation Division. Death is naturally commonplace in a war zone but there are other crimes perpetrated within military ranks—homicide, desertion, robbery—that fall under the CID's jurisdiction.

McGavin wore a snubnosed .38 revolver in a holster at the base of his spine, concealed by his shirt. He was thirty-two years old, dark-haired and heavily muscled. He wore black slacks, black shoes and a black shirt, blending him in with the night.

Saigon, the nation's capital, once called the Paris of the East, with only two predominant religions, Buddhism and Christianity, was a bustling metropolis of over two million people, becoming more overcrowded with a daily influx of refugees from the war-torn countryside. Yet Saigon remained a city of wide Parisian boulevards, lined with trees and outdoor cafés as well as a labyrinth of mean, twisting Asian streets that were more like alleys.

McGavin had chosen one of these streets for his approach to this deserted spot of deep shadow on the waterfront, having navigated his way through a cadre of prostitutes along Rue Martine. He'd selected that route because he could pass unnoticed amid the hordes of civvy-wearing American servicemen who frequented this red-light district even though it was off-limits and occasionally swept by US military police.

Vietnamese women are considered by many to be the most beautiful women of Asia, small-boned, generally blessed with petite breasts and a shapely figure, raven-black hair, creamy brown skin and catlike eyes. These traits were on display every step of the way. The working girls of Rue Martine, posing provocatively against storefronts or under the glow of corner streetlights, were clad in everything from skimpy halter tops and Western-style hotpants to mid-thigh leather skirts and unbuttoned blouses. Lascivious offers were openly called out to the vehicles crawling by on the crowded street and the offers whispered huskily to pedestrians like McGavin. GIs roamed in packs, laughing and drunk, surveying the goods on display.

McGavin had not been distracted. He was on a job. A job that could turn deadly in a heartbeat. That was his only concern at this moment. He wouldn't have been tempted anyway because McGavin had a wife back home in the States who, in McGavin's opinion, put every other woman on the planet to shame, regardless of nationality or anything else. He only paid attention to what was behind him, to make sure he wasn't being followed.

Those times when he did allow himself to think of Kelly, safe back home in the Real World, he had to admit his heart would ache with loneliness for her. There had been his leave times when she'd met him once in Perth and again in Sydney. They'd spent most of their time loving up a storm with the *Do Not Disturb* sign on their door.

During their separation, while he was in Vietnam, McGavin's wife had continued the rise through the ranks of professional photographers that she had been on when they first met in New York. Kelly was two years his junior, a redhead with intelligent green eyes that could glitter mischievously. At five-foot-two she had a firm, in-shape figure. In the three years since their marriage, she had never been your average military-base wife.

Cord was supportive of her career. Not only supportive, he was also damn glad that the woman he loved was far, far away from this world of war that was his daily existence. And so, he had not been even a little tempted by the garish display of flesh for sale as he made his way to the waterfront.

Ten minutes after he had arrived and positioned himself behind the old rotted wooden post, Major Lahn Cho arrived, wholly unaware of McGavin's presence. There were no street lamps nearby but even in the indirect illumination of the passing river traffic, Cho's erect bearing could be clearly discerned. He began pacing at the far end of the pier.

Major Cho wore civilian clothes, a casual polyester shirt and slacks. He would be armed. The creaking of the rotting boards at that end of the pier carried to McGavin through the sounds of water washing against the pilings. McGavin knew the man well enough to know that Cho would be impatient but not nervous. The man projected competence and an aura of physical strength even across this distance on a dark night.

Those qualities had earned Cho his reputation as one of the toughest, most efficient investigators in the Army of the Republic of Vietnam's military police. The South Vietnamese military was referred to by Americans by verbalizing its acronym, ARVN.

He and Cho had worked together on cases that had required cooperation between the investigative branches of the US Army and the ARVN. Such overlapping jurisdiction was not uncommon. The CID also had a paid informant inside ARVN headquarters which is how McGavin had learned that Cho was planning to meet someone here at this place at this hour. McGavin wanted to know more.

A small boat materialized out of the night. Someone seated in the stern worked an outboard motor, guiding the craft in to where the bow bumped gently against the pier.

Something *was* going down here . . .

McGavin shifted his weight, drawing his pistol. The humidity made the .38's grip slippery in his fist.

He vaguely discerned a figure stepping from the boat onto the pier. The boat was now obscured from his line of vision, so he had no way of knowing for sure how many were aboard the craft. The figure that had stepped from the boat straightened on the pier to face Cho. They spoke in Vietnamese across a gulf of some twenty feet.

McGavin had learned enough Vietnamese to get by but he could not hear them. At that moment, on the river, a passing ship's horn bellowed.

Before the echoes of the ship's booming horn had dissipated, angry saffron flashes stabbed at each other on the pier.

The man from the boat fired first but his shot had gone wild. By the time he fired again, Cho was throwing himself down flat and returning fire with one, two quick shots. One or both rounds hit and sent the man toppling backward over the end of the pier. The splash of the body hitting the water was clear enough.

A second figure leaped from the boat onto the pier to open fire at Cho. This one also missed because Cho became a rolling figure, seeking cover behind a piling across from the shooters. Cho resumed returning fire.

The exchange of pistol shots made a dull popping sound in these open spaces with all of the clamor of the surrounding river noises.

McGavin left his concealment to assist. Cho was a

brother officer under fire. But he'd only advanced a dozen paces when new action flared.

A vehicle—a panel van, lights off—burst from a nearby alley, where it had been waiting, as if shot from a catapult. The van squealed to a stop at the opposite end of the pier. A side door popped open and a pair of commando-like figures jumped out armed with rifles.

They opened fire.

Chapter 2

....

The distinctive hammering of M16s on auto fire tore apart the night and the weapons' muzzle flashes flared up into the night like strobe lights. But the two from the van were firing downrange at Cho. They had not yet spotted McGavin.

It was one hell of a wild shootout. Cho was pressing himself to the pier and firing after the boat that was speeding away down river, even as he himself was taking fire from the men in the van.

The gunmen were silhouetted by light from inside the van, making them easy targets. McGavin started squeezing off rounds from his .38. Both bullets hit both targets. One took a head hit that knocked him off his feet and back into the van. The other guy caught his in the gut. Holding onto his rifle, he doubled up, toppling to the ground.

The van's tires squealed, kicking up a cloud of burnt rubber. The van sped away.

McGavin's peripheral hearing indicated the gunfire at the other end of the dock had ceased.

He rushed to the fallen gunman, an inky figure curled up in a fetal ball with a spreading pool beneath him that was black and shiny like an oil slick. McGavin snatched up the M16, prying it loose without effort from unresisting hands.

The guy was in pain, gasping for air.

"Oh, Jesus. Oh, sweet Jesus . . ."

McGavin raised the M16 to sight in on the fleeing van. The vehicle was fast approaching a narrow side street that led away from the waterfront. McGavin triggered an extended burst of auto fire that dotted a pattern across the rear of the van seconds before it gained the intersection.

The van wobbled crazily, slacking its speed but still traveling with plenty of momentum when it plowed into the jutting corner of a towering brick warehouse. There came the thudding impact of crushing metal, the shattering of glass. Then the gas tank exploded. The van disappeared into a bursting fireball that sent debris clattering to the nearby pavement.

McGavin lowered the M16. The man at his feet had stopped gasping and crying out. He was dead. McGavin was on one knee, confirming this with a vain attempt to detect a vital sign, when Cho came stalking over to him.

Cho had not holstered his pistol. His eyes flared with anger.

"You! McGavin! What the devil are you doing here?"

His accent bespoke tutoring in English by an Etonian Brit. The clipped, upper-crust accent was brittle with unsuppressed fury.

Down the street, flames licked at the nearly unrecognizable remains of the van. The hint of roasting flesh wove into the unpleasant tapestry of the muggy night.

McGavin said, "What the hell are you pissed off about? I just saved your life."

Cho's mouth was tight. He holstered his pistol at his hip where it was concealed by his shirttails worn out in the Asian fashion.

"I repeat, by whose authorization are you here?" The Etonian accent remained brittle, quivering.

McGavin set down the M16 next to the dead man. He then confirmed something he suspected by inserting two fingers beneath the throat of the dead man's black shirt. He felt the tell-tale shape of American dog tags.

"Damn," he said softly. Then, to Cho, "Later for the hostility, Major. We should work together on this. You just stepped into a setup tonight. Tell you what. I'll tell you why I'm here if you tell me why your here. What do you say?"

Cho made a rude sound.

"You think I need American arrogance on my side in order to succeed?" His gaze lifted from the dead man to the van's flames that were beginning to subside. "You have shut off the last source of information I needed in an investigation that has been operational for six months."

"Simmer down," said McGavin. "You're lucky to be standing there breathing. And it's thanks to me. We could work this out together, Cho."

Glaring beams of light suddenly engulfed the scene, originating from half a dozen ground-level and rooftop positions. Military vehicles raced in to converge on the area from either direction. ARVN vehicles, with rooftop lights flashing, disgorged uniformed soldiers who hustled double time, some toward the smoldering wreckage of the van while others established a perimeter.

Cho said, "They call you Americans cowboys." He spat the word. "I call you nothing but arrogant and trouble. You possess no sense of true discipline. You exhibit no respect. You come to our country and make it your country's personal battleground. What happened here tonight . . . your involvement is *not* appreciated."

"Now wait a minute, Cho—"

"I do not have the luxury of waiting. I must salvage what I can of what has happened. Your interference in ARVN activities, in my investigation, will be reported to your superiors."

Cho spun on his heel and stalked off toward his subordinates.

McGavin said under his breath, "Well, I'll be damned."

Chapter 3

....

Colonel Ambrose slammed his fist down on his desktop. "You're a cowboy, goddamn it, that's what you are. A goddamn cowboy!"

McGavin said, "That's what Cho said last night."

Ambrose sighed mightily. The detachment CO was fifty years old with creased, leathery features and a salt-and-pepper crewcut. Sturdy and compact of build, he glared at McGavin who stood smartly at parade rest before him.

"Well, Cho was right on that score, at least, and maybe on a whole lot more. But we'll likely never know thanks to your unauthorized intervention. Cho's screwed-up big bust has put a damper on CID-ARVN relations, to put it mildly."

McGavin's fatigues were sharply pressed. His boots boasted a shine that reflected the morning sunlight pouring in through the one window of Ambrose's office at CID Headquarters. McGavin had exchanged last night's concealed .38 for a Colt .45 automatic holstered at his hip.

"They'll get over it," said McGavin with a dismissive shrug. "ARVN will need our forensics lab or our Interpol connections soon enough."

Ambrose chuckled grudgingly. He leaned back in his desk chair.

"McGavin, you're incorrigible. But I would like to know what the hell you were doing down on the docks of Rue Martine last night."

"Uh, Colonel, is the ass chewing over?"

"Yes. As you were, Major. Take a load off, McGavin. We need to talk this out."

McGavin pulled a wooden back chair around and sank onto it so he could lean forward, resting his weight on the back of the chair.

"Ready to talk, sir."

Ambrose said, "The dicey part is you killed an American soldier last night. Maybe three of 'em, for crying out loud. The second shooter and the van driver haven't been ID-ed yet. But that is what could land you in a world of shit."

"What was the soldier's name?"

"Specialist Fourth Class Leo Wertner of Topeka, Kansas. Twenty-six, divorced, no dependents. Assigned to his unit's motor pool. I've got people poring over his personnel file as we speak but so far, nothing."

"I'll tell you something and you can take it to the bank," said McGavin. "The Army's better off without him. And you're kidding about me being in shit, right? That puke was firing on me and Cho when I dropped him. They were trying to kill Cho. The bad guys had set him up."

Ambrose made a placating gesture.

"Relax. Even if Cho is a dick about it, any shit coming our way out of this should be minimal."

"That's more like it."

The colonel produced a pack of cigarettes, fired one up with a Zippo and extended the pack to McGavin, who shook his head, no thanks.

He'd given up smoking. It hadn't been easy but it had been the single condition Kelly had insisted on before agreeing to marry and cohabitate. He hadn't been tempted by a cigarette since.

The thought brought Kelly's image to mind. McGavin generally thought of his wife several times a day and he now felt relief again that Kelly was not a part of his world here in Vietnam. Her work as a photojournalist was hard-hitting and obsessive but generally not of the dark byways of human degradation and twisted souls into which McGavin's investigations invariably took him. Nor would she ever know the side of him that could pump a round into a son of a bitch and not only feel no remorse the next morning but consider it a service to his country.

Even here in the air-conditioned comfort of the colonel's office, he was damn grateful Kelly would never know or have to experience this side of him. Her work was hard-hitting but McGavin considered her safe regardless of what she was up to as long as she was back home in the World.

Ambrose exhaled a thin stream of gray smoke at the ceiling.

He said, "As far as those dead GIs last night go, the sad fact is that from time to time a GI is found with a couple of bullets in him or his throat slit and his wallet gone in that part of town. For now, Cho's people are letting us handle the connection of our people being involved."

"I'm surprised they gave you that much."

"They had to give us something, so that's the bone they threw."

"What's Cho's version of last night?"

The lines around the colonel's eyes deepened. "I haven't spoken to Cho yet today or last night."

McGavin tugged at an earlobe. "Maybe the direct approach would have worked better," he conceded. "I should have gone straight to Cho and asked him what he was working on."

Ambrose leaned forward and crushed out the half-smoked cigarette, squashing the butt in the ashtray more than was necessary.

"You should have come straight to me. You never will learn the rules."

"Sir, I thought you were done chewing me out."

"I guess, in your case, it comes naturally to me. Dammit, McGavin, if it weren't for the fact that you're the best damn investigator I've got—." Ambrose interrupted himself with an irritable wave of his hand. "Oh hell, why can't you learn how to play by the rules like everyone else just once?"

"I'm going to make a serious effort to learn Vietnamese. Will that do?"

"The way I'm feeling right now about you, McGavin, any change would be an improvement."

"About the two in the van, the other shooter and the driver."

"Charcoal," Ambrose said. "Burned beyond recognition. Dental records are being traced but we won't have that for another day or so. Now, are you going to tell me why you were so interested in Major Cho that you ended up caught in that crossfire?"

"I've been picking up rumblings."

"Rumblings."

"On the street," said McGavin. "You know how it is, sir. Like on the street back in the World." McGavin had been a detective in Chicago. "Nothing straightforward, not connected directly to anything I'm working on. Just whispers. Bits and pieces of chatter popping up here and there. Little tangents from cases I am working."

"And what do these rumblings tell you? To trail an ARVN colleague to some dark pier on the waterfront after midnight?"

"It was a drug bust gone haywire," said McGavin. "Cho was about to make it when the bad guys tried to take him out first with a double cross of their own. I was there just to eavesdrop and ID the players for future reference for my work, which is more and more involving drugs. Homicide, theft—drugs are nearly always involved."

"Drug use in-country is reaching epidemic proportions," Ambrose agreed with a nod. "Reefer's the least of it. Heroin. Speed. Morphine. It's bad enough here in the city. It's worse out in the bush."

"Until now," said McGavin, "the problem has been use by Army personnel. But the rumble is that this is something bigger than that coming together. If the dots connect the way they could, we're talking about Army personnel dealing in drugs wholesale from Viet suppliers. That's bad enough but I think they're also shipping the stuff back to the World for distribution on the streets of American cities."

"But you didn't think of reporting that to me?"

"Rumbles," McGavin repeated. "I've got nothing tangible, only what I've put together from whispers on the grapevine. Nothing actionable. I guess that's what I was looking for last night."

Ambrose found and lit another cigarette.

"McGavin, I'm going with you on this because you've never gone wrong before, not once. So, okay. Rumbles. Rumors. Something said here, the piece of a puzzle there, and trailing Cho last night was because you got wind he was onto something big going down on that pier." Ambrose played absently with the Zippo as he spoke. "Looks like you were right. Cho is royally pissed off. He's not taking or returning my calls and that's breaking SOP right there."

"We do have a secret line into their office, right?"

"We do and that's another reason I'm letting you ride on this. I spoke with our contact a short while ago. The dots are being connected, Major, from what I've managed to get and from reading between the lines of what Cho's spokespeople are putting out. Those rumblings and Cho's bust are connected. But I'm still pissed that you didn't come to me about it. Do you always have to play cowboy?"

"I guess it did backfire this time," McGavin conceded.

"I guess it did. ARVN had enough to initiate an investigation. Cho must like your style. He was playing cowboy too. He thought he had the pieces connected just right and he had it put together last night for a nice, tidy bust. That is until things, as you say, went haywire."

"What about the guy Cho shot, one of two who showed up in that boat?"

Ambrose took a final drag on his cigarette before crushing it out in the ashtray.

"His office is saying that the body was washed away and not recovered. Who knows? That's why Cho slapping the lid on things is so damn aggravating."

"He is on the right track and so am I," said McGavin. "American GIs and Viet drug dealers going into business together. They teamed up to wipe out Cho. It was a pact between them so they knew they could trust each other. And if Cho was worth all that trouble, he sure as hell was onto something big. So where does that leave us, Colonel?"

Ambrose said, "It leaves you off the case."

McGavin's eyes tightened. He sat up straight in the chair.

"Say that again."

"You heard me. The word I am getting from the Viets is that Cho won't even consider a friendly working relationship with us until you've been taken off this case."

"I thought we'd dismissed his ability to screw my career over what happened."

"We did," said Ambrose. "But I've got to work with the guy, dammit. ARVN feed us intel too, you know, from their moles in the Vietcong ranks and from their informants in the cities. Yeah, your ass chewing is done, Major, but I'll state another fact for you. I'm pissed at Cho, him not sharing his intel with us since it involved American servicemen." Ambrose patted his pockets, frowned when he realized he was out of cigarettes. "I'm trying to work a compromise here to keep everyone happy."

"Permission to speak freely sir."

The colonel broke eye contact and ran a leathery hand

across the salt and pepper crewcut.

"Permission granted."

"Sir, everyone gets screwed with a compromise. I'm a soldier. I live to win or lose. Compromising goes against my grain."

"You think I'm any different?" asked Ambrose. "The difference is I'm the one manning the helm and taking that heat. Dammit, I've got to keep Cho happy and keep running this part of the green machine. You're off the case, McGavin."

"You mean I'm off the rumbles. There hasn't been a case yet, right?"

"That's the way it is for now. It's better than giving you what Cho wants and that's the ax. I'm doing you a favor, son. Take it. I've got something else in mind for you."

"And if I hear any more rumbles?"

The creases deepened in Ambrose's features.

"Bring them to me. Nothing is set in stone. I want to take down the bad guys as much as you do. But I have made it clear, have I not, that your cowboy shit will cease?"

"Yes, sir. So I'm not getting transferred and you're structuring for a brighter day with Major Cho. And you've got something in mind for me."

Ambrose paused to lean back in his swivel chair. He stroked his chin and a hint of amusement warmed his eyes.

He said, "I'm assigning you a partner."

McGavin said, "Something must be wrong with my hearing, sir. It sounded like you said, 'partner'."

Colonel Ambrose opened a desk drawer and withdrew a manila folder, which he set on the desk before him.

"The Pentagon is undertaking a second front in this war."

"Second front? Where? Against whom?"

"A war for the hearts and minds of the American people." Ambrose's countenance grew serious. "You've heard about the war protests back home."

"I've heard."

"The Pentagon is on a campaign to grant the news media access to military operations. I guess the big brains think that if we're in their living room on the TV news every night and if we're all over *Time* and *Newsweek* and their daily newspapers, folks will start rooting for us again instead of marching by the hundreds of thousands to end the war. At least, that's the plan."

"It stinks."

The colonel made another check of his pockets, still not finding a cigarette.

"I know. That's not the point."

McGavin said, "They'll see the war in their living rooms and their newspapers. They'll put that together with the body bags coming home and they'll never stop protesting until it's over."

"The point," said Ambrose, "is that I've been ordered to supply someone from this detachment, an operational field officer, so a stateside photographer who's been assigned to this detachment by Washington can follow the officer around for, oh, a couple of months and photograph everything the officer does in the line of duty."

"Me, huh?"

"Afraid so, Major." Ambrose went so far as to give a wink of satisfaction. "You've been giving people big-time headaches lately. Now it's your turn. I'll sort things out with Cho. In the meantime, you back off from Cho and go about your normal assigned day to day duties. And you will be accompanied by a stateside photographer."

"I don't like it, Colonel."

"I didn't think you would, Major." Ambrose glanced at his wristwatch. "Your photographer is due in on a Philippine Air Lines flight from Manila at 1100 hours. I suggest you shake a leg."

McGavin knew when he was licked.

"I'm on it, sir. Does he have a name, our photographer? Do we have a picture I can use to identify him?"

"We do." Ambrose flicked open a folder on his desk. "The name is Carpenter. And it's not a he, it's a she."

McGavin grumbled, "This is a man's war."

Ambrose flicked an index finger through the file's onionskin pages.

"Her authorization to full access is all in order," he noted. "First name, Terry, Toni, tuna, something like that. Ah, here it is. Kelly. Kelly Carpenter."

McGavin became aware of a skip in his heartbeat. He cleared the catch in his throat.

"Did you say Kelly?"

"That's right. Has a whole list of credits and references. Impressive and not a bad looking gal either. You could do worse." Ambrose slid the folder around, opened to the section paper-clipped with a face-front and profile photo of the subject. "Take a look, McGavin. Meet your new partner."

McGavin stepped over to the desk on legs that felt like they were made of wood and did not want to move. He looked down at the photograph with eyes that wished they could look at something, anything else.

The familiar features of his wife stared up at him and even in the flatness of the black-and-white photographs he could detect the inherent mischievousness and insatiable curiosity and determination that made Kelly such a powerful woman, as strong in every way as she was beautiful. He stared down into the ambitious, determined eyes of the woman he loved and made an effort not to exhibit visibly what he was feeling inside.

He pulled his eyes away from the photograph and said, "I'd better get to the airport and meet her."

Chapter 4

....

The PAL flight from Manila to Saigon was a half-hour late. McGavin spent the time waiting in an air-conditioned cafeteria, sipping iced tea.

Tan Son Nhut Airport was busy, as usual. In addition to a steady flow of waiting, departing and arriving US military personnel—some in transit alone, others as units—there were the civilians. McGavin overheard people chatting in at least half a dozen languages. There were Europeans interspersed with Asian businessmen, Vietnamese women attired for travel in traditional neck-to-ankle dresses, slit up to the waist with silk pantaloons beneath. There were wispy-bearded taipans from the Cholon Chinese district of Saigon, in their stiffly elegant, brocaded robes, accompanied by entourages of body-guards and personal assistants.

He was at the gate when her flight landed.

Kelly was the third passenger to disembark from the plane. He saw her stepping down to the tarmac before she saw him. She reminded him of fire and ice, there in the glaring sunlight and heat that made most people look pale and wilted as they scurried for the air conditioning. Not Kelly. She wore tan slacks, a white blouse, and stylish, functional flat-heeled shoes. A camera gear bag was slung over one shoulder. She carried a leather suitcase that McGavin recognized as one that he'd bought her two Christmases ago.

Then she saw him. She did not smile or wave but strode toward him with the look of someone expecting to face the music. As she approached, everything around them faded for McGavin except for her.

She moved with the long-legged, confident gait of an independent, strong-willed woman. Sunlight made her red hair a halo. She had a peaches-and-cream complexion, high cheekbones, and lush lips, and, because she never wore makeup, you could see the freckles smattered across the bridge of her nose. Gorgeous and radiant, she possessed a figure that belonged in a men's magazine.

Despite everything, something stirred in McGavin's loins as always when he saw her. That's when he knew he had a problem.

Saigon was a city of daily random acts of violence perpetrated against Americans. Constant vigilance and an awareness of one's surroundings were essential. To have that awareness dulled, which was the effect this woman had on him, could put them both at risk.

The city's base crime rate wasn't much greater than any city of a proportionate size anywhere. The differ-

ence was that armed combat raged across the Vietnamese countryside. Many of the urban acts of violence were
motivated by politics, not greed or poverty as elsewhere.
Teams of Vietcong, young men and women in civilian
clothing, scouted the streets on foot and on wheels, search-
ing out Americans to kill them. Along with bombs planted
in night clubs and movie theaters frequented by off-duty
GIs, the war too often reached into the city.

There was uncertainty in her eyes when Kelly reached
him.

"Cord."

"Kelly *Carpenter*?" he said.

She eyed him closely.

"Do I get a hug?"

"Not yet. What the hell are you doing here, Kelly?"

"If we can't hug, can we sit down somewhere and talk?"

"Yeah, that's a good idea. Some explaining is in order."

He took her suitcase and steered them to the dining
area where he'd nursed his iced tea. They found a corner
table where a wide window overlooked the runways. A
passenger jet was just completing its takeoff. McGavin ordered another glass of tea. Kelly ordered coffee.

"Okay," he said after the waitress retreated beyond
earshot. "Let's hear it."

"You're really upset with me, aren't you?"

"Let's put it this way. It takes a lot to throw this soldier,
honey, but you have pulled it off in grand style. I can't even
think of the word to describe what I felt when my CO
showed me your picture and told me about this."

The corners of her mouth curved up with the hint
of a smile.

"Dumbstruck?"

"What?"

"That would be the word to describe how you felt."

"Do us both a favor," he said quietly. "Dispense with the levity. What the bloody hell is going on here?"

"Okay. I couldn't tell you what I was up to before this, Cord, or I wouldn't have stood a chance of getting to Vietnam. You'd have seen to that."

"You're damn right about that. I'm listening, Kelly. I don't hear anything."

She sighed. "Here it is in a nutshell. I have gone through considerable finagling, including a cockamamie story for my editor about the need for a cover name, to get this assignment: to be a photographer assigned to accompany you on your assignments."

Another momentary pause as their orders arrived.

"First, the basics," he said when they had their privacy back. "Why the name change?"

"Twofold. I had to play the system, Cord. I needed to slip in between the cracks. I had to. You know about my new job with the wire service."

Damn, he thought. She'd mentioned it several letters ago and he, in turn, had offered his congratulations and the promise to celebrate with a special dinner the next time they were together. They had been exchanging weekly letters since his deployment. Kelly's career as a photojournalist, notably her feature for the *Washington Post* on ghetto life conditions within blocks of the White House, had attached her name to the buzz word *Pulitzer*, earning her a staff position for one of the major wire services that provided photos to news media outlets around the world.

"And the wire service sent you here?"

"Exactly."

"So why are you Kelly Carpenter?"

"I didn't want special treatment because of the Pulitzer talk. I didn't want to stall out in General Westmoreland's headquarters and listen to official blather. I'm here to cut through that. I want the real stuff."

He said, "You changed your name because the Army brass would never assign you to me in a million years if they knew you were my wife. They might even balk at you being in-country altogether while I'm assigned here."

"Cord—"

"There's a reason they wouldn't have assigned you to your own husband. Want to know what it is? The best edge I've got going for me in this world I live and work in is that I am a cold, mean-ass son of a bitch without a god-damn thing to lose. They need men like that, with nothing at stake because, that way, we deliver and anyone on the other side who does have something at stake will end up either running for his life or dead."

"And you think that with me here, that will change?"

"What the hell do you think?" he rasped. "I love you, woman. I'd stop a bullet for you. And with you at my side through the kind of lowlife, dangerous work I deal with in a war zone, I very well could end up losing my life, taking a bullet to save yours. I wouldn't hesitate. And if I did that, the work I should be doing won't happen and that will be because of you. Frankly, hon, I'd call that damn unpatriotic and selfish behavior on your part. What would you call it?"

Her eyes lowered.

"I guess I'd agree with you if I thought of it in those terms."

"Well, try thinking in those terms, why don't you?

I'm a soldier and this is war. For me, what other terms are there?"

"There are the people back home," she said. "There are the American people whose interests you and the military are supposed to be serving over here, whose husbands and sons and brothers and fathers comprise the military. There are too many body bags coming home, Cord, and not enough progress over here to show for it. I'm here to take photographs of the *truth* and I want someone I trust—I mean really, *really* trust—to show me that truth of what's happening here."

Politics was the only area in which their relationship was not always harmonious. That had never seemed important to McGavin in light of the chemistry that fueled them in every other department . . . until now.

He said, "I should have said that war protesters are the stuff Pulitzer prizes are made of."

"Cord, we've been over that before. I'm not going to argue with you, you dinosaur. I'm also here because I love you."

"Is that right? Darlin', you've got to be the curve-throwingest woman I ever did know."

"You love my other curves too," she said with a twinkle in her eye. "I saw that first look you gave me just now when I walked in and, mister, I've got the same look for you."

"Knock it off. That was lust. I haven't had a woman since the last time I saw you. But you were saying something about love."

"Cord, I got restless."

"Women are born restless. Kelly, please. It meant something to me, knowing you were on the other side of the world, safe from what's going on over here. That the very thought crossed my mind this morning, a few minutes before my CO showed me your picture and explained that you were my next duty assignment."

"I'm sorry, Cord, but you knew when you married me that I could never be the little woman tucked away back home, keeping the home fires burning. I, uh, don't imagine you told your commanding officer who I really am or I'd be under military arrest, right?"

"Keep explaining."

"I couldn't stay in the States and keep on loving you without really knowing what you're going through and who *you* are. It's as simple as that."

"But you know me better than anyone."

"I know one side of you. I know the caring, tender, compassionate, strong side of my loving husband. But it's time I learned more. I deserve to know everything about you."

"Is that so?"

"Getting assigned over here seemed like a good opportunity. That's why I went through the bureaucratic contortions and cover story gymnastics, the name change and everything else. That's why, Cord. Bottom line, is it's about you and me."

"Sounds more like it's about you and nobody else."

"It is about us," she said. "It's about that wild, cold look I see flash in your eyes for just a heartbeat when something happens that really offends you. Like the time you stepped in and stopped that guy when he was about to get physically abusive with his date in a restaurant, remember? We ended up giving her a ride that night to her mother's. Or that time we saw a man kicking his dog in the park. Remember that?"

"Kelly, have you considered that you'll interfere in my career, tagging along with that camera of yours?"

Her green eyes remained unsure but with a sense of relief at something she heard in his voice.

"Oh Cord, I know you can blow this whole deal for me if you want to but please, *please* don't. Why should you be against the citizens back home learning for themselves what's going on over here? As far as interfering with your work, I just won't allow that to happen. I'd never have done this under normal circumstances. But this war is hardly normal, wouldn't you agree? I'm here to experience it and that will allow me to know you completely. Is that so bad? Work with me on this. Only good will come of it."

McGavin finished his iced tea. He set the glass down on the Formica tabletop with a clunk and studied Kelly without saying a word for thirty seconds. She wore the look of a defendant awaiting the verdict, which, it occurred to him, is exactly what she was.

He said, "I'd be taking a real gamble on you, hon. I should go straight to my CO and blow this gig right from the git-go."

Her wariness became steely.

"That would not be good for our marriage, Cord."

He chuckled.

"I was wondering when you were going to play that card."

"My mind is set on doing this. It's just that it would be so much easier on both of us if you don't ruin it or make me regret it."

"I think you'll end up doing that on your own," said McGavin. "Okay, let's try it your way. I'll go along with this insane charade and let you pull the wool over their eyes."

Her expression shone at first with wariness, not relief.

"For real? Don't play a trick on me, Cord."

He tugged at an earlobe.

"It's like this. I'm too good for them to court-martial or otherwise can. This morning, someone with juice in the ARVN wanted me yanked because of something that went down last night, and Colonel Ambrose deflected it nicely in my interest. So, I figure no matter what happens with you, the worst it can get for me is another dressing down from the CO and that's gotten to be a weekly occurrence anyway. I don't have anything to lose. Here's the deal. Call it male ego. That should please a feminist girl like you."

"I'm not a girl, I'm a woman," she said mildly.

"I don't want to be made a fool of. All right, you win the first round. I sealed my fate when I didn't say anything to the colonel when he first showed me your picture and handed me this assignment. Now I would look like a foolish, duped, stupid husband if I turn you in or I can count on figuring some way through the complications if they do tumble on to who you really are and that I'm in cahoots with you."

She reached across the table, her fingertips brushing the back of his hand.

"All I want is to take pictures, Cord." She spoke as softly as her touch. "I've worked the streets in the States. I covered police vice and drug operations and I never got in anybody's way."

He felt a tic in one eye which he quelled, hoping she had not caught this reflexive indication of the electricity that jolted through him at her slightest touch.

"Let's make that the case here. Stay out of my way,

Kelly Carpenter, in the performance of my duties. And I don't want contact with you when we're off duty."

"Ooh, I'm not sure I like that," she said, her palm resting across the back of his hand. "I don't mean to be unladylike, darling, but I was hoping that we could, um, steal some moments alone together for—you know?"

The temperature seemed to climb in the air-conditioned cafeteria. McGavin knew it was only him . . . and her. He drew his hand away.

"You're not going to want to see much of me after I tell you the rest of the deal."

Her brow furrowed.

"And that is?"

"I reserve the right to make every effort to convince my CO that, officially, I don't want you assigned to me and I think you should be sent back to the States. I'm sorry, hon, but I don't want you over here on the front lines. That's just the way it is. You get to stay and I'll keep your secret like the complete idiot I am. But if I do persuade them to transfer you home, you're gone. That's the deal."

"Do I have a choice?"

"Not a one. Pulling a harebrained stunt like this, you're lucky to have any deal from me."

"Yes, I suppose I am. All right, Cord. We have a deal."

"Then let's get started."

He had regained his sense of inner equilibrium. It was easier when he wasn't feeling her touch. His body temperature returned to normal. He rose from the table, picked up her suitcase and stalked from the cafeteria.

Kelly hurried to keep up.

Chapter 5

....

They drove through Saigon without speaking at first. The tarp roof of the open-sided Jeep shielded them from the midday sun but not from the heat or the sensory overload of their surroundings. The heat was like an invisible choking fist, squeezing the lungs. The combined dust and smog fumes tasted coppery.

Teaming boulevards and narrow inland streets overflowed with coursing humanity, thousands of pedestrians, bicyclists, and people on every manner of vehicular contrivance. The traffic was a cacophony of noise and rabble. The streets were overhung with telephone and electrical wires, the gutters stacked high with garbage. Impatient, chattering, beeping throngs pushed and shoved through the steam bath humidity.

Kelly's eyes grew wider with every passing mile. She

snapped photographs while McGavin concentrated on driving conditions that worsened, reducing their progress to a stop-and-go pace. They became completely stalled out in a dense traffic jam no more than ten minutes from CID Headquarters, the Jeep snared in mid-block with vehicles bumper-to-bumper ahead of and behind them.

That's when McGavin caught movement in his outside rearview mirror:

An oncoming motorbike driven by a young woman in a dress with the traditional conical hat so common in-country. A teenage male riding behind her on the motorbike. The automatic pistol he held was clearly visible as the motorbike raced in on the left side of the Jeep.

"Get down," McGavin snapped at Kelly.

He flung himself at her, gripping her shoulders, tugging her roughly with him down as low as possible, his nostrils so close to her tangled red hair he couldn't miss the tantalizing scent of her jasmine perfume.

Automatic gunfire opened on them, drowning out the young man's angry screams in Vietnamese. Bullets pinged off the Jeep's chassis, zipping through its tarp roof. The motorbike went whizzing by.

Kelly gazed up at McGavin across the half-inch separating their eyes.

She said, "Are you really a filthy, imperialist pig like he said?"

McGavin's thought process skipped a beat.

"You know what he said? You speak Vietnamese?"

"Part of my prep. I've been taking a course five nights a week for six months."

"Well, I'll be damned. Excuse me, hon. I've got to return fire."

He brought himself up, tugging the .45 from its holster. The motorbike was picking up speed, still no more than a couple of car lengths ahead. Tracking the pistol up to take aim, he could still—

Then something else caught his attention in the Jeep's rearview.

Another motorbike! Speeding in from behind. Two males riding this bike. The backup team. A classic one-two setup. The passenger was taking two-handed aim at the Jeep with a machine gun.

Kelly was reaching for her camera bag.

McGavin said, "Stay down!"

He swung his .45 into target acquisition before the gunman on the second motorbike could trigger his weapon. McGavin's bullet kicked the guy from the back of the bike to the pavement where he rolled several times and then did not move.

Panic was in the motorbike driver's expression as he sped past. McGavin tracked his pistol around and squeezed off a careful shot. This kid toppled wide-armed from the bike and the riderless motorbike stormed on and crashed through the plate-glass window of a storefront.

McGavin leaped to the pavement. He saw the riders of the first bike stalled out only four vehicle lengths ahead, finding themselves blocked in by this noisy traffic jam even on a motorbike. McGavin raised the .45, then held his fire. Rubbernecking citizens weaved back and forth everywhere. He could not risk hitting an innocent bystander.

The motorbikers saw this. A break in the traffic jam presented itself and they changed course toward the mouth of an alley across the street.

McGavin said over his shoulder to Kelly, "Stay put."

He bolted from the Jeep, not looking back, his focus on nothing but hot pursuit on foot.

As the young woman, who looked to be no older than twenty, angled the bike for the alley, the kid on the back twisted around, shouting more insults and rage in Vietnamese at McGavin. He fired another burst. Several of his countrymen caught rounds and dropped while everyone else scrambled for cover.

McGavin bounded over the hood of a truck. He ran toward the gunfire, gaining speed, bounding across obstacles as if they weren't there, closing in just as the motorbike roared into the alley.

By the time he reached the mouth of the alley, the motorbike was halfway to the opposite end of the alley and the parallel street, its engine's racket magnified by the confines of the alley walls like a chainsaw gone berserk. McGavin had no taste for killing a woman and he wanted one or both of these two alive for questioning. He aimed carefully and fired a single shot, low.

His bullet struck the bike's rear tire. The motorbike veered sharply into the nearest wall, colliding with it at maximum speed, tossing off both riders.

The female flew through the air, upside down, to strike a metal dumpster.

Her passenger tumbled to the pavement, rolled twice and jumped to his feet. He hadn't lost hold of his weapon. Seeing McGavin stalking into the alley, the kid brought the weapon up to fire.

McGavin fired a single shot from the hip. The bullet caught the gunman in the abdomen. The Viet doubled over, the pistol falling from his hand. He took two backward steps until a wall stopped him. He collapsed facedown upon the pavement with no sign of life in him.

McGavin peered beyond the motorbike's wreckage. The driver lay sprawled upon the filthy pavement alongside the dumpster. Her conical hat, tipped forward, concealed her face. Her broken neck was twisted at an impossible angle.

Detecting movement advancing behind, McGavin whirled, the .45 tracking up. He froze. He was drawing up a bead on Kelly.

She stood there busily snapping pictures of McGavin with the carnage-strewn alley as a backdrop, rapidly-clicked shots of the demolished bike and of the dead girl with the broken neck.

McGavin lowered his pistol.

He said, "Let's start with war zone 101, shall we? It is not a real good idea to come upon a man's blind side during a firefight."

While he spoke, Kelly shifted the camera to photograph the gut-shot teenager.

"I waited until the shooting stopped," she said defensively, turning to address McGavin directly. Then she froze. *"Cord, look out!"*

McGavin's eyes and .45 swung around toward the direction she'd indicated.

The Viet kid who'd driven the other motorbike came stumbling into the alley. His left hand tried in vain to stem the blood flowing freely from his side. His pockmarked features burned with pain and hate. His right hand was filled with a pistol leveled at McGavin.

Without hesitation, McGavin tackled Kelly, knocking her from the line of fire while simultaneously triggering a round that caught the young man between the eyes and blew his brains out the back of his head. McGavin landed atop Kelly as the gunman dropped.

Lying there atop his wife, McGavin's ears rang in the sudden silence that seemed absolute in the wake of so much enclosed violence. His remaining senses were filled with this unexpected closeness of Kelly.

Every curve of her was flush beneath him—firm breasts that never needed a brassiere (though she always wore one out of a sense of propriety), the pliant curves of her waistline, trim hips tapering into legs that could have graced a dancer, shapely, the musculature well-defined.

He felt body heat connecting them like magnets. For one crazy second, he could have sworn he felt her heart beating against his own. Before he could right himself, Kelly wrapped her ankles around his and looked up at him.

"Hello, big boy," she whispered mischievously into his ear.

He again regained his mental faculties.

He said, "Honey, it sure would be nice if you could at least survive the drive to headquarters. It'll look bad on my record if you don't."

Untwining his ankles from hers, McGavin rose to his feet. Kelly stood with him because his left arm remained around her waist and she had no choice. He stood with the .45 up and ready to blast. His eyes scanned both directions.

Traffic remained stalled on the street where he and Kelly had been ambushed only moments earlier. There was a moderately moving traffic flow on the parallel street. Pedestrians hurried by at either end, eyes front, staring straight ahead, going about their business. A few curious pre-teen children gathered at one end of the alley, jabbering and pointing.

Kelly made no effort to struggle in McGavin's embrace. She forwarded the roll of film in her camera.

She said, "If they sent two hit teams, why not a third?" She snapped a wide frame shot of the bodies and smoke rising from the remains of the motorbike. "And why aren't there any sirens? Why aren't people curious?"

"They don't want to be killed," said McGavin. "They're trying to survive in a city at war. No one will call in what just happened. Not these days in Saigon. We're in the clear. If there was a third team, they'd have hit us by now."

"So, what do we do?"

"We walk the rest of the way to HQ. It'll be faster and just as safe."

"You mean *un*safe. What about your Jeep?"

"It's the Army's Jeep. Rank has its privilege. That's an old Army proverb. I'll have the Jeep sent for or what's left of it after the street thieves get it stripped."

McGavin lowered his .45 but did not holster the pistol. His arm left her waist but he continued to guide her by clasping one of her hands in one of his. They walked away. At the end of the alley, opposite from where the curious children gathered, Kelly paused to cast a final glance at the dead bodies.

"What about . . . them?"

"Let the local cops clean it up if they want to."

McGavin holstered the .45 before they emerged from the alley onto the parallel street. He did not relinquish her hand, keeping her close to him as they joined the colorful flow of pedestrian traffic along the sidewalk. They almost collided with a woman gracefully balancing a cage of squawking chickens on her head, on her way to or from a market place.

As they hurried along, Kelly said, "Cord, I know you're in charge and as a civilian, I'm supposed to do as I'm told. I didn't back there just now and I can tell you're pissed about it. But, uh, I did save your life when I saw that kid with the gun, didn't I?"

"I wouldn't have had my back to him if you hadn't come on me."

She sent him a concerned sideways look.

"This doesn't change our deal, does it? You won't tell your commanding officer about us?"

"I'll keep my side of the deal," said McGavin. His eyes stared straight ahead as he negotiated their way along the crowded, busy sidewalk. "I won't tell them *who* you are, Kelly. But I'm not about to make this easy for you."

"Fair enough," said Kelly.

Chapter 6

....

"Let me get this straight," growled Colonel Ambrose, having heard McGavin's recap of the ambush. "You simply and merrily strolled away from the scene of a crime, leaving behind four people left dead by your own hand?"

McGavin stood leaning against a window frame in Ambrose's office.

Kelly sat in one of the chairs facing the colonel's desk. She had managed to touch herself up with a minimum of time and effort. Sitting in the colonel's office, she appeared fresh and composed.

McGavin said, "They weren't people, sir. They were Vietcong."

"Cho would love to hear that. One of those four might have provided useful information."

"Not unless the VC changed their SOP overnight.

Their command structure is airtight. We and Cho know that for a fact. The hell with Cho. He'll get over it and the Saigon cops are a bunch of bought-off incompetents so the hell with 'em."

"Look, we're not going to get into a turf war with these people," said Ambrose. "The point here is that you could at least make an effort to play by the rules. You should not have left the scene of that ambush. As a professional cop, you know better."

"My orders were to escort Miss Carpenter here safely," said McGavin with a nod to Kelly. "Mission accomplished."

Kelly asked, "Who is Cho?"

McGavin grunted. He said to Ambrose, "You see the problem, sir? The lady's got an inquisitive mind."

Kelly said, "It goes with being a journalist." She sent McGavin a withering glance. "I'm a reporter. I'm here to report."

Ambrose had seemed enchanted by Kelly as any male would be upon first glimpse. He eyed McGavin with some amusement.

"Uh, she has you there, Major. You and I have previously gone over this. Why are we discussing it again?"

Kelly interjected, "I do hope you gentlemen have worked out the details." There was mild reprimand in her tone. "The assignment I'm on does have Pentagon approval. This has come down through the chain of command to you, Colonel, and to Major McGavin. I don't wish to cause difficulty but it should be understood that my duty here is to report what is happening."

"We accommodated the Pentagon," said Ambrose. "But I do ask that you consider Major McGavin's concern which, despite his rather warty exterior, happens to be valid. Please remember, Miss Carpenter, the Major is the one asking questions while conducting an investigation. You will confine your activities to taking pictures, nothing more. Is that understood?"

"It is. Thank you, Colonel."

McGavin said, "Here's what needs to be understood. Major Cho is onto something big. When he gets over his hurt feelings, we'll be friends again and, if his case involves US service personnel dealing in contraband, he'll have to work with us. However it breaks, I'm going to be a busy man. I formally request that Miss Carpenter be reassigned to another investigator. How about Toomey?"

Ambrose sent her a smile, an implicit plea for understanding.

"The Major doesn't much care for compromise."

Kelly said, "So I've noticed."

"I'm here to fight a war," said McGavin, "not babysit civilians."

Ambrose glared at McGavin, no longer amused.

"The subject is closed, Major. We are done going over this, you and I. Whether you like it or not, Miss Carpenter's presence here *is* part of the war effort."

"Not *my* war effort. Any green-behind-the-ears civilian is in *way* over their head in the world I live in. I don't want her blood on my hands." He paused for a smile at Kelly. "No offense, ma'am."

Her green eyes flared.

"Well, plenty of offense taken, buster." She addressed Ambrose in a reasonable tone. "Sir, this needs to be cut and dried if this stands any chance of working the way it's supposed to."

"You'd like to see me cut and dried," said McGavin.

Kelly said, "Am I in or out?"

Ambrose sighed. "You're in, ma'am. Uh. Welcome aboard. Sorry about this inauspicious beginning."

"Let's call it memorable," said Kelly. "I've already taken some great pictures. Major McGavin is a perfect subject."

McGavin felt his eyebrows draw together in a frown.

"Subject, eh? Okay, you've had enough warnings. I won't feel responsible when something bad happens because of this crazy experiment."

"Assignment," she said patiently.

Ambrose raised both hands in a placating gesture.

"Knock it off, the both of you. You'd think the two of you were married, the way you squabble. McGavin, your mission is to show Miss Carpenter your job . . . and like it."

"I'll follow orders," said McGavin. "I'll show her my job. I'll start liking it when she's on a plane back to the World." He cleared his throat. "Uh, to change gears, sir. If I'm off the case on the river last night, mind me asking who you're handing it to?"

"You weren't on a case last night," said Ambrose, "because, as of yet, there is no case. You didn't have anything except rumbles, to use your terminology. In other words, so far we have nothing to work with. That will change once communication with Cho is restored. To answer your question, Toomey is taking over and will pick up any loose ends that show up on that angle."

"Toomey?" McGavin grimaced. "Toomey is an idiot."

Kelly said, "Excuse me, Major, but if that's true, why did you want Toomey assigned to cover me instead of your more-than-competent self?"

"Apples and oranges," said McGavin. "Toomey is a fine spit-and-polish example of the CID at its best when it comes to routine work. Right, Colonel?"

"He's no idiot," said Ambrose.

McGavin cleared his throat and said, "He almost got me killed on that bust we worked together last month."

"So, Toomey isn't the brightest bulb in the barracks." Ambrose shrugged mildly. "But he's between assignments. And relax, Major. If anything really solid comes in, it will be through my pipeline into Cho's office, not from street rumbles."

"Shows how long you've been off the street, sir," said McGavin, adding, "with all due respect. So you're saying those rumbles I picked up are going on hold with CID initiating no follow-up investigation at this time?"

"We're talking about decisions made above my rank and pay grade and you know it," said Ambrose. To Kelly, he smiled. "And ma'am, I expect you to regard these inter-agency politics as strictly off the record, of course."

"Of course, Colonel," Kelly said without hesitation.

Ambrose said to McGavin, "And who the hell knows what you were picking up? If there's anything out there, something will come across my desk. And when it does, you'll get it. Maybe."

"What about the tracer on those dental records from the van?"

"The roasted guys were a muscle head PFC from Alabama and a street punk, also Private First Class, from Detroit. So far, about all we have is positive ID."

"What do you mean, that's about all?" said McGavin. "What about the guy those three bunked with? What did they have to say?"

"Funny you should bring that up," said Ambrose, "because that happens to be our next order of business. See, they bunked four to a bay in that detachment's living quarters. The three dead guys were cooks, serving up slop—" he interrupted himself with deference to Kelly, "— I mean army chow, in the mess hall."

"Three dead guys?" Kelly repeated.

They ignored her.

McGavin said, "And what is our next order of business?"

Ambrose slid a manila file folder across his desktop.

"Your next assignment. Get started on it ASAP." He looked at Kelly. "I guess that means it's your first assignment in-country too, Miss Carpenter."

Kelly charmed him with a smile.

"I'll do my best," she said. "Mouth zipped shut, eyes and ears open."

McGavin said, "That'll be the day." He picked up the manila folder. "What have we got?"

"The fourth guy who shared the bay with those three you creamed is an AWOL meathead named Cates. In view of what happened to his roomies, we've upgraded his status from Absent Without Leave to Desertion and that's the job I'm dropping in your lap." He eyed McGavin with a small grin. "Is that enough of a bone to toss your way, Major?"

"It'll do." McGavin picked up the file. "So I'm not off the case."

Ambrose nodded. "You're just out of Cho's hair until he cools off."

Kelly was watching McGavin as if her eyes were taking pictures. She said nothing.

McGavin flicked open the file folder and glanced

through it. Specialist Gerald Seymour Cates was Caucasian. Regulation crewcut. Large jug-handle ears were his only distinguishing characteristic. McGavin became aware that Kelly was looking over his shoulder, studying the photograph. He snapped the file shut and dropped it back onto the desk.

Ambrose said, "Cates is a company clerk. He's the one among the four who had access to inside information. So he could be part of it. Along with the CO and First Sergeant, the company clerk is privy to just about everything that goes through the orderly room of any consequence unless it's highly classified. He routes ARVN and Viet civilian matters to the CO along with everything else. That's the connection between Cates and those three guys who went down last night."

"Thank you, Colonel."

"You want to thank me?" said Ambrose. A flash of emotion flared in his eyes and voice. "Then track down that son of a bitch Cates. Track him down and bring him in. I don't like deserters. Let's hear what he has to say about Major Cho and what went down last night. He's been spotted in the Little Texas section, at a place called Kandy Kane's."

"I know it," said McGavin.

"Thought you might. So get on it."

"Consider it got," said McGavin.

McGavin exited the office without a backward glance, trusting Kelly "Carpenter" to keep up with him.

Kelly remained good to her word and said nothing. When they emerged from the air-conditioned headquarters building into the stifling afternoon heat, she was at his side.

McGavin decided to see what she was made of even if he already had a pretty good idea. He waited until they had passed the sandbagged machine-gun emplacements around the main entrance. Then he broke into a double-time trot down the sidewalk in the direction of the parking lot.

Kelly clasped her camera bag to her side and gave chase.

* * *

Colonel Ambrose stood at his office window, hands clasped behind his back, watching the woman hurry after McGavin. It was a pleasant, if momentary, diversion from the rigors of a busy day. He saw no reason to let the moment pass without savoring his view of a woman's well-shaped backside as he hadn't seen one in some time . . . at least beyond the glossy airbrushed fantasies of the girly mags so prevalent in a man's war.

This woman was one hundred percent real, a fine-looking beauty in motion. Not just a woman but a *white* woman. You didn't see many of those in Vietnam these days! Ambrose had to admit to himself that his admiration for what he was looking at was, really, nothing but pure lust. Or maybe impure, considering the wedding ring on his left hand.

But what the hell, he told himself. Any man would want a woman like the one he watched hurrying along the sidewalk that passed below his window. He was man enough to admit it.

Ambrose hadn't seen his wife—in fact, he hadn't seen America—in decades except for the rare, brief holiday visits now and then. He was a military lifer, plain and simple and proud of it. He'd enlisted as a twenty-year-old farm kid the day after Pearl Harbor and had gone on to become part of the big push that liberated Europe from Nazi tyranny.

He'd drawn a role in Germany's reconstruction after the war, raising him higher through the ranks with its power and prestige. Then came Korea and then peacetime postings to various points around the globe, some glamorous like in Rome and some not so glamorous like Guam. And, through it all, he had remained upwardly mobile through the ranks . . . until Vietnam.

As he neared retirement age, much of where he went next would be determined by what happened here in the Nam. Of this, the colonel was acutely aware.

And the war was not going well.

The Vietcong's sweeping Tet Offensive of eighteen months earlier had dealt a severe blow to the US military and in terms of prestige and credibility. That, coordinated with North Vietnamese series of attacks on more than one hundred South Vietnamese cities and outposts, had succeeded in heightening communist resistance and rebellion in the countryside and in the cities.

In Saigon anyone who could work a hustle had it going down full-tilt. In volume alone, the crimes assigned to the CID for investigation were mounting daily. Murder. Theft. Black market activity. Drugs. And all of it landed on the colonel's desk. *On the other hand though,* thought Ambrose, *some elements of this could work in our favor.*

The woman and McGavin rounded a corner of the building in the direction of the motor pool, disappearing from sight.

When Ambrose turned from the window, his thoughts lingered on them. He took considerable pride in possessing a well-proven ability to gauge and assess character and nuance. He was pretty damn certain McGavin would locate the missing Cates. *But what was going on between McGavin and the woman assigned to shadow him?*

Several investigators in the colonel's detachment had been cops in civilian life. McGavin was the best of these. Yes, he would find Cates. That wasn't the question. The question was: What *exactly* was the nature of that interesting energy Ambrose sensed coursing just beneath the surface between McGavin and the woman?

The colonel intended to find out.

Chapter 7

....

McGavin had made arrangements with the motor pool before taking her to see Ambrose. He climbed behind the wheel of the waiting Jeep, identical to the first.

Kelly settled into the passenger seat just as he was gunning the engine to life. She was slightly out of breath, her forehead glistening with perspiration from the exertion of having kept up with him.

She said, "That wasn't a very nice thing to do."

"Neither was you flying over here and screwing up my job."

She regarded him with a lifted eyebrow.

"I got the impression you're in hot water with this Major Cho about whatever happened last night. Three dead? That's the other side of you I was talking about, Cord."

He glanced over his shoulder and shifted the Jeep into

gear with enough force to jar her so hard that she had to grasp the Jeep's metal frame to keep from tumbling out. He steered from the parking lot, cutting toward a side street that abutted the base, a shortcut he preferred to reach the front gate.

He said, "So you and I are working together. But never forget, Kelly, I don't like it and I resent it. I don't like you being on the front lines, not one damn bit."

"Well, get over it, McGavin," said Kelly with a roll of the eyes. "You're sweet to care so much about my safety but those are your orders and that's the way it is. And it could be worse," she added with an unexpected, playful lilt to her voice. Reaching over, she rested her left hand on his right leg just above the knee. "You could have gotten assigned to a woman who didn't turn you on the way I do."

Again, her touch was like an electrical jolt, sparking his pulse, making his throat go dry and his loins grow warm. He brushed the hand away.

"We already went over this," he said. "Jeez, will you please get it through your head. Stop trying to mess with me."

He then made a show of keeping his full attention on the sparse traffic.

This was his third tour of duty in The Nam. It sometimes seemed like several lifetimes since his Basic Training at Fort Leonard Wood. AIT had been in helicopter maintenance, Green Machine logic in action given that, as a former police officer in civilian life, he had absolutely no knowledge of helicopters. But he proved to be a good student, learning fast and more than what he needed to know. He'd even taken a few joyrides, piloting a helicopter now and then when the CO wasn't around. Then they shipped him off to Nam, assigned to a field maintenance unit.

He was the best helicopter mechanic there was but not for long. Destiny stepped in. The VC attacked the outpost where he'd been temporarily stationed during a routine repair job on a crippled chopper that needed work before it could make the return flight home. The "engagement" was twelve hours of bloody slaughter. During that time, McGavin took various actions under fire that saved lives and took the lives of more than a few VC. This resulted in the battlefield commission that ended his work on helicopters and eventually, because of his civilian law enforcement career, led to his present MOS and duty assignment. Green Machine Logic. There was nothing like it. The solving and resolution of several significant cases had raised him through the ranks.

During his tours of duty in-country, McGavin had gradually and reluctantly come to believe that the American public, not to mention the armed forces, had in many ways been sold out by short-sighted, misinformed and/or corrupt politicians back home. The soldiers in Nam were fighting the good fight, fighting their guts out in a war that in many ways, for a variety of reasons—logistical, political, and cultural—had been unwinnable from the outset. That American servicemen fought so valiantly in spite of this only served to heighten McGavin's heartfelt respect for every man who served while at the same time heightening his moral disgust for the self-serving politicians who sent good men and boys to die in a war that likely should never have been waged in the first place.

And now Kelly shows up . . .

But dammit, McGavin had to admit she looked mighty fine in his peripheral vision, her red hair wild in the cross-draft passing through the moving Jeep.

An empty troop carrier drove past, heading in the opposite direction, away from the airfield. They passed a lone sentry, eyes posted front with a rifle at port arms, before one of a row of looming aircraft hangers. There was no one else in sight in the immediate vicinity. They continued past the first hangars.

Kelly suddenly reached over with both hands and yanked the Jeep's steering wheel, guiding the vehicle abruptly into a narrow, high-walled canyon formed between two of the towering, unoccupied structures.

McGavin braked the Jeep in the shaded area and turned in his seat to give Kelly a piece of his mind. Before he could speak, she pressed herself to him and their bodies melded. His mouth, opening to speak, received her steamy kiss and he found himself responding with equal fervor, embracing her. When the kiss broke, they gulped air in deeply like two people submerged underwater for too long.

Her cover girl features were flushed, flustered.

"My God, Cord. How I've missed you! I didn't think this would happen. I mean, not so soon. But baby, I've been *missing* you!"

He managed to slip the Jeep into gear and shut off its engine. The activity of the sprawling military complex around them, beyond the hangars, disappeared. Their lips locked again.

Her tongue darted sensuously, penetrating, caressing his tongue. Her teeth nibbled his lower lip and that sent McGavin's body temperature soaring. Maintaining the clinch, he leaned across her, pressing her back against the seat, and half mounted her as best he could, considering that they were fully dressed and restricted by the confines of the Jeep. Kelly slumped down to facilitate his maneuver.

McGavin placed a hand to the front of her blouse, cupping her left breast, palming it with firm gentleness. He positioned one of his knees against the material between her legs and began applying pressure there with the knee. Kelly clamped her legs around his knee, shifting her thigh this way for only a few seconds before her entire body began to quiver and tremble in his arms. She moaned.

"Oh Cord, I've missed you so much!"

McGavin heard himself admit, "I guess we both needed this."

Her body still quaking, she placed a hand over his, guiding his hand beneath her blouse to the lacy coolness of an unseen brassiere. He knew what she liked and began tweaking her nipples through the thin material with his thumb and index finger. Kelly moaned again and her hips again bucked uncontrollably with a spasm. This, combined with the touch of her lace-covered breast and the way she rubbed her clad thighs against him, caused McGavin to groan, and he shuddered with the explosion of his own release.

When the intensity of the brief moment passed and their bodies began to relax, he heard Kelly sigh a happy, almost girlish giggle.

"Now that, Cord, is what I call a real reunion between husband and wife."

"Oh, really? You mean making a grown man, a military officer on duty no less, shoot a load in his pants like a schoolboy?"

Her green eyes sparkled. Despite reality's inevitable intrusion and the return of rational thought, McGavin found himself planting an affectionate kiss on the tip of her nose.

"In the future I'll try not to force you into anything against your will." She retrieved a traveler's packet of tissue from her purse. "Here, honey," she said sweetly. "I think you could use these."

Chapter 8

....

After "personal matters" were tended to, McGavin backed the Jeep out from between the hangars and they continued on.

An uncertain silence stretched itself between them.

McGavin did not know what to say or what to think about what had just occurred. On the one hand, it was a relief to have the sexual tension acknowledged and, of course, there had been the physical pleasure of it. But he was concerned at how little willpower and restraint he'd exhibited.

They made one stop, after leaving the base, before going to little Texas. McGavin first drove to a neighborhood of residential back streets. There was a vaguely European ambiance to the neighborhood, a remnant of the long-ago French occupation: a working-class section of quiet alleys flanked by wooden houses, some with bamboo fences and others standing flush against the street's edge.

"I keep a place of my own off-post," he explained. "I like having somewhere of my own that no one knows about."

"A love nest?"

"Hardly. I've been faithful, hon."

"I know you have. I'm sorry for kidding about something like that. You're a man who needs his own corner to draw into. I've always tried to provide that for you."

"You have. Over here, I've had to provide it for myself. I spend four or five nights a week in my quarters on-base. Off-duty time belongs to me. A lot of the guys head off-base for their downtime, though a lot of them don't."

"After that ambush this morning, I can see why they wouldn't."

They drove past two bright red pillars, the vermillion gate of the neighborhood Shinto shrine. Kelly snapped pictures. A little farther on, they passed an old man wearing a conical hat, drawing a battered wooden cart heaped high with rags. She spoke between camera clicks, sighting the Minolta and snapping away.

"Are you breaking regulations by having a place off-post?"

"No, though I am breaking a few by not letting my CO know about it. But that's okay. Ambrose can run the detachment without me for a few days here and there."

"The colonel seems very capable."

"He's a by-the-book, spit-and-polish soldier. I like that."

McGavin eventually braked the Jeep to the curb before a modest old house that, like most of the others in the neighborhood, was built of wood with a roof of curving, upturned eaves.

Kelly lowered her camera in her lap, studying the house.

"Why bring me here and show me this place if it's against regulation?"

He shut off the Jeep's engine.

"Two reasons. First, because I know my secrets are safe with you."

"Of course they are. I'm your wife."

"Right. A lot of good that's done me in getting you to do what you're told. No, honey, the way I see it is that you've got a heck of a lot more to lose than I do in the secrets department, so mine are safe with you."

"Well, thanks for your vote of trust." She replied with only a trace of sarcasm and started from the Jeep. "Do I get the twenty-five-cent tour?"

McGavin reached over to rest a hand on her left leg just above the knee, checking her progress.

"Another time," he said.

A red eyebrow arched.

"Messy house?"

"No, you'd approve. I just don't want to be trapped in there with you and have to fight off your sex drive."

She gave him that look she always did when she wasn't sure if he was kidding.

"Cord—"

"You heard the colonel." He stepped from the Jeep. "I'm working. I don't need any more distractions. I'm stopping for a change of clothes. We're hunting a fugitive on his own turf." McGavin indicated his fatigues. "He'll get word that I'm in the district before I can even pick up his scent if I go in looking like this. Wait here."

Kelly settled back against her seat with a throaty chuckle that sounded to McGavin like clean mountain water gurgling across smooth stone. She folded her arms primly.

"All right, the little lady will sit patiently and wait."

"Right. I've been waiting for that since you showed up."

She watched McGavin walk away. Something about the way he moved reminded her of a jungle beast, all sinew and muscle. Grace and savagery combined.

She thought, *Maybe tonight*, and had to bite her lower lip to hold back a chuckle at her lasciviousness.

They had taken to each other right off. Cord McGavin was a genuine, nice guy. Her kind of guy. You could talk ideas with him, not just about the weather and the price of eggs. He was a thoroughly competent individual with emphasis on the *individual*, tough enough to wade through fields of fire without succumbing to the dehumanization of combat that could erode the strongest and best of men.

They were kindred spirits. Their opinions differed on enough things to offer lively conversations, which they both enjoyed. They had a mutual respect for each other's intellect. They agreed on most of the important things and enjoyed each other's company. Oh yes, there was lust, but they had, over the course of their marriage, also managed to become very good friends.

He reappeared five minutes later, his fatigues traded in for a civilian shirt, slacks and shoes with a lightweight sports jacket that concealed the shoulder-holstered .45. He had phoned for a taxi, which arrived with reasonable promptness.

The driver didn't need directions once McGavin said, "Little Texas," and they were off.

Chapter 9

....

Little Texas was a tawdry red-light district adjacent to Duong Tu-Do, Liberty Street, a busy boulevard that bisected Saigon. It was a noisy, neon-saturated world of civilians, troops, gangsters, deserters, refugees and black marketers, where white boys from the country and cities back home came to let off steam, get liquored up and patronize the vast array of sex dives that existed only to clean their wallets with the help of naked dancing girls, gambling and whores. A red-light district frequented by off-duty *black* enlisted men was a nearby Harlem-on-Saturday-night section called Soul Kitchen.

Although the American military was integrated, the off-duty leisure time of most soldiers was not. Martin Luther King had been assassinated only two years earlier. Even the concepts of integration and the civil rights movement were less than a decade old. These were times of social upheaval and one result was the deepening entrenchment of prejudice. The racial divide in the States represented by the riots, the burning cities, was reflected in Vietnam—a muted but unmistakable racial divide. There were exceptions, considering the many who were serving in-country, but generally it was a fact of life that most white soldiers frequented establishments like brothels and sex clubs that catered to them while black GIs did the same.

The cabby let McGavin and Kelly off in front of Kandy Kane's which was situated on the ground floor of a three-story brick structure set back from the street. Its ornate ironwork around the windows was a nostalgic holdover from the days of French colonialism.

A Viet barker stood on the sidewalk in front of the club.

"In here, folks! Right this way!" The heavy Viet accent and bantering delivery made for a surreal, comical mix. "Prettiest girls in Saigon! Passable food! Cheap drinks!" When McGavin and Kelly stepped by him on their way in, he prattled, "Excellent choice, dear hearts! Have a good—"

The rest was lost beneath the din of recorded rock music that vibrated the floors and walls of the smoky club.

Kandy Kane's was doing good mid-afternoon business with patrons lined three-deep along an American bar that ran the length of the place. A large mirror behind the bar gave the illusion that the club was twice its size. Rock music emanated from speakers strategically placed behind small stages upon which curvaceous young women danced, each with her own pole about which they wrapped their trim, scantily-clad bodies like lewd, provocative serpents. Encouragement from the drunks in the crowd nearly equaled the recorded rock music. In addition to servicemen, a few couples occupied the row of tables along the opposite wall with hardly enough room to bend their elbows.

McGavin took Kelly's hand and led her through the crowd. He tipped a hostess to get them past a velvet rope and into a paneled and carpeted, more dimly lit dining area with discreetly distanced booths and tables. Their table provided a good view of the action but was well removed from the cacophonous noise near the bar. The tables here were occupied by lunching business-men and a smattering of couples. A pretty Viet waitress came over and was only mildly surprised at their order of two Coca-Colas.

The direct route for McGavin would have been to go straight to the club owner and inquire about Cates since he was known to be a regular here. Viet civilians invariably cooperated when American military investigations spilled into the private sector. Not to cooperate only drew heat from the local government and no businessperson in Sai-gon wanted that. McGavin had no idea if Kandy Kane was a real person, man or woman. He knew about this place only because it was his job. He had never worked the vice detail, so this was not within his primary area of operations unless an investigation took him to a place like Kandy Kane's. He was also conscious of treading cau-tiously here because of Kelly's presence.

But with a link established between Cates and the three who'd died violently last night on the waterfront, there was every reason to think that Cates, too, would be near here. There was a good chance he was in favor with the owner or manager, whoever he or she might be. He'd likely be warned if McGavin openly inquired about him. As for the likelihood of his presence here, the very fact that Cates had been sighted in this joint even though he was wanted for desertion—a charge punishable by death—placed the deserter squarely in the profile of a man addicted to such places.

Kelly cast a bemused glance about them.

"Knew right where to bring me, didn't you, soldier? Are you sure this is work?"

McGavin chuckled. "If it wasn't, I'd take you to a classier dump than this."

"Well, thanks for that, anyway."

McGavin grew serious. He began scanning for every GI face among the patrons, starting at the front.

"Our mission is to find Cates if he's here," he reminded her.

Kelly said, without pointing but indicating with a nod, "There he is, bussing a table at the rear toward the end of the bar."

And damn if she hadn't spotted him, paying attention with her photographer's eye at Cates' photograph back in Ambrose's office.

It was Cates, alright. Jughandle ears on either side of a beefy, flat featured face topped with a crewcut. The deserter had, apparently, worked his way into the good graces of whoever ran this joint thanks to his long-time patronage. The idiot must've thought he was in pig heaven, not only hiding out from the MPs but getting to watch the dancing girls jiggle up close.

McGavin said to Kelly, "Stay here," and sprinted from their table.

He un-holstered the concealed .45, his jabbing elbows, heft, and unstoppable momentum rudely pushing a way through the crowd with no consideration other than getting to Cates. He shoved aside inebriated servicemen who cursed him until they saw the gun and then made way for him amid shouts from the dancers and the audience at the sight of a gun-wielding man charging past.

Someone was dashing after him in his wake. Kelly. She would be "un-holstering" and readying her camera.

Cates looked up from his task and saw McGavin storming toward him. He bolted. Kelly lifted her camera and snapped a picture. The indoor flash caught Cates rushing out through a metal bar-push door, McGavin less than ten feet behind him and closing fast.

The flash revealed no one coming to Cates' aid. Bouncers and bartenders remained at their stations. No one except Kelly was giving chase. With everyone assuming this was some sort of personal matter, no one wanted to get involved.

McGavin powered through the doorway after Cates, keeping low in case the guy was waiting outside to open fire.

There was no gunfire. Cates was running down a narrow walkway in the direction of the busy street fronting the club. This end of the walkway was blocked by a wooden fence. Cates hadn't gone a dozen steps when a delivery truck backed up to the loading dock of the next building, blocking that route of withdrawal for him as well.

Cates looked back and saw that McGavin had been delayed scant seconds by crouching when he first came through the doorway. Cates used this bought time to jump up and grab hold of the bottom rungs of a fire escape ladder above him. Easily hoisting himself up, he started to climb without another backward look, scrambling upward past a second-floor line of windows.

McGavin gained the ladder, holstering the .45 in order to grip the bottom rung of the ladder and begin his climb in hot pursuit.

Kelly hesitated at the bottom of the fire escape. She couldn't help but note that Cates scrambled like a frightened mouse fleeing a hungry tomcat, whereas Cord negotiated the twists and turns of the ladder like a stalking beast in pursuit of its prey, unimpeded by man-made obstacles.

She thumbed off the camera's flash mechanism. She didn't need the flash outdoors. There was plenty of sunshine. And she didn't want to distract McGavin. She snapped off three quick shots of Cord and Cates nearing the top of the fire escape, McGavin again closing the distance.

She lowered the camera by its neck strap. She attempted a leap, only to miss her reach for the bottom rung of the ladder. She cursed quietly, fervently, and tried again. This time her twice-a-week gym workouts paid off. She seized the ladder just as the boys had, hoisting herself up to climb after them, grunting with more exertion than she would have liked.

So, this was Cord's reality! Adrenaline pulsed through her, as did her concern for the man she had come halfway around the world to join. Yes, it made for great photographs. That was a purely automatic, professional reflex on her part. It's what she'd come to see: Cord in action. Great pictures, without a doubt. But something more than adrenaline drove her up that ladder. There

was violence in the air. She felt it. Someone could die
here at any second.

She thought, *Cord, be careful!*

Above, Cates scrambled onto the roof, McGavin close
behind him. McGavin vanished from Kelly's sight, bounding from the top of the fire escape onto the roof.

Kelly climbed faster, less than twenty seconds behind
them.

Chapter 10

....

By the time McGavin made it from the top of the rick-
ety fire escape onto the roof of the building, Cates had
reached the center of the roof. He whipped around, drawing a concealed pistol and aiming at McGavin.

McGavin flung himself down. A gunshot. The bullet
whizzed over McGavin's head. He triggered his .45, not
aiming for Cates' torso or head but for his legs. If Cates
had information about what happened on the pier last
night—and there was damned good reason to believe that
he did—McGavin wanted him alive.

Cates moved faster than expected, darting the rest of
the distance across the roof after firing, and McGavin's
bullet missed as Cates vaulted, without stopping, across
the chasm of ten feet that separated this building from the
roof of its closest next neighbor.

McGavin bolted to his feet, aware of Kelly behind him. She'd made it up the fire escape and was now also on the roof. He thought, *Stay safe, hon!* He picked up his pace, also leaping across the chasm without hesitation.

This neighboring rooftop was sloping, tiled. The soles of McGavin's shoes and his free hand fought to gain traction but he started sliding downward. He ground his knees against the tiles. His weight and the fabric of his slacks stopped his skidding before it could gain momentum and send him over the edge. Having gained traction, he peered up to see Cates scramble awkwardly across the tiles, up and away from him like a crab scuttling across a beach. He almost gained the peak of the roof, throwing a frantic glance over his shoulder at McGavin, his eyes wide, panicking orbs.

McGavin lifted his .45 skyward and triggered a round. The *crack!* of the heavy caliber report was commanding up here in the relative quiet of the rooftops.

He shouted, *"Freeze!"*

Cates disappeared over the peak of the tile roof to the other side.

McGavin scrambled after him. Something was driving the deserter more than fear of arrest. Cates was behaving like a cranked-up druggie. Only a very frightened man keeps going in the face of a blasting .45. Even the stupid respect a gun. A fear greater than that drove Cates. McGavin was curious to know what it was. Was it tied in with those "rumbles" he'd been instructed to forget? McGavin topped the roof peak.

Cates was sliding down the tiles on the far side into a free fall that landed him atop the roof of the next building over, a single-level structure. It was a one-level drop, and in the process of maintaining his balance, he lost hold of his pistol. The gun dropped to the ground between the buildings. Cates picked himself up. He saw McGavin sliding down the first roof after him. Cates ran toward the kiosk of a roof stairway.

McGavin propelled himself away from the slanted roof, becoming airborne for a few seconds, his arms extended. He plowed into Cates and, with about seventy pounds on the guy, took the deserter down with a *thud!* and a mighty exhalation of breath from Cates. McGavin rolled and landed on his feet.

Cates regained his balance, hesitating on his knees. His eyes took on a reflexive belligerence.

He said, "No need for roughhousing, general."

"Don't be a smart ass, sonny boy," said McGavin. "That's my advice, so take it. You're outranked. I'm Major McGavin."

Cates' features were a ghostly pale. A club-life-and-hard-drug complexion. His accent was Dixie. North Carolina.

"So okay," Cates sneered. "You ain't a general. Piss on ya."

He started to rise.

McGavin, holding the .45 down at his side, felt sweat beading on his forehead.

He said, "Stay where you are, punk. I don't like working hard in this heat."

Cates remained in a kneeling position, eyes uncertain.

"So what the hell am I supposed to do?"

"I'm working at tying you into something that went down last night. It concerns those three yahoos you bunk with."

Cates licked his lips nervously.

"What about 'em? I hardly know them guys."

"You were tight with them. The four of you thought you were real badasses. You do know they're dead, right?"

"Yeah, yeah, I heard about it."

"I'm the one who killed them."

Cates' Adam's apple bobbed.

"I tell you I don't know nothing about them guys, Major. You just now busted yourself a deserter. Take me in."

McGavin smiled a tight smile without humor.

"You're scared to death, Cates. What are you afraid of? Come on, you can tell me."

"Like hell I can. I don't trust no one. I'm not saying a damn thing."

"Then I'll make sure of that," said McGavin.

He swung his right arm in an arc. The barrel of the .45 slapped Cates upside the head. Cates eyes rolled in their sockets, showing the whites. His knees buckled. He started to collapse. McGavin hurriedly holstered the .45. Stepping in, he lowered a shoulder and caught Cates, preventing the fall. Cates was snoring. McGavin effortlessly flung him over his shoulder in a fireman's carry.

Kelly stood there observing, springy on her feet. Her red hair was tangled. She raised the Minolta and snapped a picture of McGavin standing there with the unconscious man across his shoulder.

"Good work, Major."

He was relieved to see her unhurt but he didn't let on.

"Thanks for shooting off that flash back in the club," he said. "Gave me a chance to size up what I was up against."

"I think they were glad to get rid of us."

McGavin started toward the roof kiosk with his human cargo.

"I had to make Cates easy to handle. Let's keep moving. That's another rule to remember. Over here it's best not to light in any one place too long."

Kelly gave a short, nervous laugh.

"I'm that way no matter where I am," she said. She stepped past him to tug open the squeaky door of the kiosk. "What do we do now? You're going to book Cates as a deserter, I take it."

"Uh-uh. This boy's involved in something more than that."

"Isn't desertion in the military the ultimate crime? What could be worse?"

"I'm not sure," said McGavin and it bugged him to admit it. "I'm working on what my gut tells me, adding that to some things I've been trying to put together in my mind. Maybe Cates deserted because something got too big for him. He wanted out. I want to get this punk somewhere where he and I can have ourselves a private chat."

"You're not going to book him?"

"Honey, whatever he's involved in has Cates scared to hell and that's got me interested as hell."

"All right, I'll bite. Where are you taking him?"

McGavin said, "I'm taking him home."

Chapter 11

....

Making their way through the narrow streets of Little Texas, they did not appear particularly out of place: a couple
out slumming with a friend, who had passed out from too
much fun and was now being literally carried home where
many a funny tale would be recalled at the Officer's Club.
That's how it would appear to any drunken servicemen
who cared enough to notice.

Once they were on solid ground, Kelly was the first to
spot and hail a passing taxicab.

The driver was a Viet teenager with a narrow face
aflame with acne, split by a good-natured, gap-toothed
grin. His dashboard radio was tuned to a station playing
Satisfaction by the Rolling Stones through a tinny speaker.

He said, "Your friend, he have too much good time,
eh?"

Kelly held open a rear door of the taxi for McGavin to unceremoniously flop the unconscious Cates into the cab. Cates fell into a corner, his slouched form remaining completely out of it, reeking of alcohol.

With Kelly seated next to him, McGavin gave the driver their destination, an intersection one block from the house he rented. Then he closed the sliding glass partition that divided the back seat from the front, positioning himself so he could watch the driver's eyes in the rearview mirror. McGavin's fingertips hovered near the lapel of his sports jacket, inches from the butt of the concealed .45.

The driver steered his taxi from the curb to join the moderate but steady vehicular flow along the boulevard. His eyes remained on the traffic. His hands remained at the formal two-and-ten position on the steering wheel. McGavin sensed no danger or threat from him.

Kelly watched McGavin watching the cabby.

She said, "After that ambush this morning, I see the problem. You can't tell who the enemy is over here, can you?" She indicated to their driver with a discrete nod. "Do you think he's VC?"

"No reason I should think that," said McGavin with a shrug. "But yeah, the enemy can be anyone: the jolly, fat mama-*san* who does the unit's laundry. The cute little kid outside the gate who gives your boots a shine. The old man standing out in the rice paddy. Friend or enemy? Any one of them could toss a grenade or bullet your way at any time.

"So how do you tell?"

"Easy. If they try to kill you, they're the enemy."

She held her purse and camera bag a little tighter than

before and sat rigidly, watching the passing scenery out-side the taxi windows, her mouth pinched at its edges.

"I can see how that would make a person very para-noid, very fast."

"Call it careful," said McGavin, then he glanced side-ways as Cates began to stir.

Cates opened one bleary eye, then the other, and then spent several seconds becoming aware of his surround-ings, of being slouched on the leather seat of a moving vehicle. He sat up.

"Hey, where the hell—" His Dixie accent was slurred. He interrupted himself, lifting his hands to his head. He said, "Oooh, my head. Who slapped John! My head feels like it's been torn plumb off."

"You were smarting off," McGavin told him, "and I didn't like it. Had to pistol-whip you, son. Don't make me do it again."

The glaze in Cates' eyes started to clear.

"Oh yeah," he said. "Oh yeah, I remember . . ." He glanced unsteadily at Kelly. "Who's she?"

"She's none of your damn business," said McGavin. "We're going to have ourselves a little chat, you and me, when we get to where we're going."

He'd never stopped eyeing their driver from the corner of his eye. The driver remained looking straight ahead, driving.

Cates remained huddled in his corner of the taxi as if wishing he could disappear. He raised both hands to cradle his head.

"All right, all right. I've got to think."

Kelly said, "You haven't done such a good job of that so far, have you, soldier boy?"

This brought a glance of disapproval from McGavin. Cates seemed not to have heard.

"What makes you think I even want to talk to you?" he asked McGavin.

McGavin said, "You will. But for now, shut up."

Cates lowered his face into his hands and began massaging his head.

Kelly said nothing, yet her keen eyes missed nothing. She snapped pictures of street scenes they passed.

McGavin leaned back in his seat and crossed his arms so as to appear relaxed as the taxi worked its way through the traffic but his fingertips never moved far from the butt of the .45. When they reached their destination, McGavin paid the driver. As the taxi drove away, he gripped Cates by an arm above the elbow. Kelly stood at Cates' other side.

Cates was completely awake by now. He watched McGavin's every move, having not spoken since their exchange in the taxi.

McGavin had chosen this intersection because it was a busy transit hub. They were instantly absorbed by a noisy sea of human activity. Buses and a trolley disgorged and took on passengers. People were walking and bicycling past with that exhausted, I-just-want-to-get-home look of the weary day worker worldwide.

No one paid them any notice.

After determining that they were not under surveillance, McGavin commenced walking without releasing his grip on Cates. Trying to keep up with his long strides, Cates tripped once or twice but did not fall. Kelly accompanied them and they continued to be, for all practical purposes, three friends out for a stroll.

The sun was setting when they reached McGavin's house. He led the way onto the quaint front porch, unlocked the front door and shoved Cates into the cozy living room that was furnished in teak and bamboo in the Asian fashion. It was a forceful enough shove that Cates went slamming into a refrigerator in a tiny kitchenette area opposite the front door.

McGavin stripped off his sports jacket.

"All right, you traitorous little puke," he said. "Now the fun begins."

Chapter 12

....

Kelly followed McGavin and Cates into the house from the porch. She closed the front door and withdrew her camera from its case.

Cates had regained his balance from having been pushed against the refrigerator. He righted himself. His eyes widened when he saw Kelly raise her Minolta.

"Hey, wait a minute. Who'd you say she was?"

"I didn't," said McGavin. He stepped between them, blocking Kelly's shot. "I told you not to worry about her. She's not your problem. I am."

"Oh no, you ain't!" Cates' words were rushed with panic. "My main concern is staying alive! Because of what I know, there are people who want me dead."

"And who would they be?"

"Bigger than you," said Cates as if regretting having to

say so. "I can slick my way out of your Army noise with a good lawyer maybe, but if I tell you what I know, I'm dead meat before the sun sets." He indicated Kelly. "Who is she, Major? I don't want no dang pictures!"

"She's a reporter from the States," said McGavin. "Pretend she's not here. That's what I'm trying to do."

Cates eyed Kelly with astonishment.

"You *want* to be here?" He was genuinely mystified. "You stupid bitch. You must be out of your cotton-picking mind." He said to McGavin, "That joint where you found me, I was fixing to let 'em get me out of the country. The Netherlands, he said, wherever the hell that is. They'd put me in an asylum, he said. But you know what, that'd be a damn sight better than being here, I can tell you."

Kelly rolled her eyes.

"You'd be *seeking* asylum, you idiot. Jesus, McGavin, you're dealing with a real genius here."

McGavin cleared his throat.

"Uh, Miss Carpenter, I need time alone with this man to properly interrogate him."

Her green eyes blinked.

"You're kidding, right? What if I just don't take pictures and—"

"I want her out of here, Major," Cates sputtered, his back remaining to the refrigerator, staring at Kelly with a mixture of fear and contempt as if she were a venomous insect. "I want her out of here before I say anything."

"You heard the man," said McGavin. "Please, Miss Carpenter." He nodded toward an archway leading to the back half of the house.

"Okay, okay." Kelly paused for a glance at Cates and delivered a parting shot. "And you know what, hillbilly? I expect you *will* end up in an asylum or worse."

She executed a modestly dramatic exit with chin raised.

Cates stared blankly at McGavin.

"I don't understand what she just said to me."

"I know what you mean," said McGavin. "I guess I've gotten used to it." He holstered his .45 and stepped forward so that he was toe to toe with Cates, towering over the shorter man. "Now, let's get back to that chat. Just you and me, Specialist Cates."

Cates gulped loudly.

"Sure, Major. Anything you say. Uh, look here. What if you promised me a safe ticket out? I mean *o-u-t* out as in cutting me orders out of Vietnam. Could you work something like that?"

"I could if it was worth my while."

"If you can get me out with charges dropped, what I've got could do you some good. Believe it, sir, it would be worth it to you if I did talk."

Several seconds passed during which McGavin's eyes frosted over. Then the fingers of his right hand clamped around Cates' throat and he lifted the guy by the neck with one arm until Cates was on his tiptoes, eye to eye with McGavin.

McGavin said, "You have information I want, dickwad. If I don't get it, I'm going to start squeezing my fingers right now and slowly crush the cartilage of your esophagus. Then I'll pour myself a drink and sit in that chair over there and watch you gag to death by inches. I don't like deserters, have I mentioned that? There's a special place in hell reserved for garbage like you, Cates. In addition to being a severe breach of military regulations, it also happens to offend me greatly on a personal level. Nod if you understand. Nod if you want to tell me what I want to know."

The suffocating, weakly-struggling man pressed against the refrigerator nodded frantically.

McGavin said, "Good."

He released his hold on Cates' throat. Cates slumped to his normal height, massaging his windpipe, taking in gasping breaths.

"Dang, Major! There ain't no reason to play rough with me."

"A point needed to be made," said McGavin. "You know what your bunkmates in that bay were up to. You were likely a minor part of it and got cold feet after I shut your pals down. "

Cates said, "I'm nothing but talk and I know it. I ain't no bad guy. I just passed along information for a cut."

"That's what I mean. You were a part of it. Why didn't you report what you knew to your commanding officer?"

Cates made a face and said, "Yeah, right."

McGavin lifted a hand. Cates flinched but McGavin, instead of raising the hand against him, placed it on one of Cates' shoulders as if commiserating with the cowed man.

"Specialist, what is it that you want more than anything else in the world?"

Cates' brow furrowed at the unexpected question.

"Uh, I dunno, sir. Well, shoot, reckon to go swimming where the gals look real nice skinny-dipping in the moonlight with the night bugs chirping. Back home where me and my buddies can go hunting and watch us some football." A wistful look touched Cates' eyes. "I don't understand none of this, Major. Why can't life be like that no more? I reckon that's what I'd like even more than going to them Netherlands Kandy was trying to sell me on if I could scare up the bread."

"Well, Specialist, I don't know about girls skinny-dipping in the moonlight but I can get you reassigned stateside. Would that be good enough?"

Cates went from looking at McGavin as the Angel of Death to looking at him as if he were witnessing the resurrection.

"But I'd need a guarantee, y'know. You'd do that for me?"

"I'd see to it," said McGavin. "So, there's your choice, puke. Tell me what I want to know or die on the floor gasping for your last breath. What do you say? Me, I'd go for telling me what you know."

"I want to believe you, sir. I really do. I want to get out of this godforsaken hellhole country alive."

"Don't we all," said McGavin. "I gave you my word, Cates. Are you in or out? This is the moment of your truth. Make the choice."

Cates looked like a man having to decide whether or not he should jump into a volcano. He exhaled a quick, sharp breath.

"It's drugs, Major. The big picture is a pipeline. US and ARVN personnel working together, smuggling drugs back to the States. Heroin, mostly. Weed ain't worth the effort."

"You're a part of that?"

"No, sir, not me. No, sir! I mean, at first this was like a one-time thing, getting them info to off somebody, some ARVN officer."

"Name?"

"I don't know, Major. Honest."

"His name is Major Cho."

"Yeah, well, I didn't want any more to do with those

guys and they were glad to see me go. Told me I'd be dead
if I ever told what I know. And I know plenty, Major, but
I ain't telling you the rest of it right now no matter what
you do."

McGavin caught a whiff of the man's b.o. He stepped
back, giving Cates—and himself—some air.

"Do you know who your bunkmates were taking orders from?"

Cates' fear had morphed into smugness.

"Yeah, I know who it is. But that's what I've got to deal
with, ain't it, Major? If you want what I know, it's going to
be on my say so and I'll tell you why."

"I know why," said McGavin. "The ARVN guys your
pals were working with won't like you being alive, flapping
your gums. You're already on their hit list."

Cates nodded.

"Right. So, you get me safe somewhere and then I'll
talk. And get this. With what I've got, I'm *only* talking to the
Adjutant General his own self. Got that? Not you, not your
CO. Only the top dog. Then, maybe, I'll spill what I know."

McGavin briefly considered his options.

He could apply field interrogation methods. With scant
effort, he could torture the information he wanted out of
Cates. But the best methods for extracting information
quickly by such means could get noisy and that could be
dicey in a residential district surrounded by civilians. Beyond that, McGavin had little enthusiasm for torture. In
the present situation, no lives were immediately at stake.

And, after all, Kelly was present . . .

McGavin said, "A private chat with the AG?"

"You heard me. Him and no one else. Make it happen,
Major."

Chapter 13

....

The colonel answered his office phone on the first ring. "Ambrose."

McGavin said, "It's me. I have our deserter in custody."

"Outstanding! Where are you? I'll dispatch a unit to take him off your hands."

McGavin stood at his wall phone, which was mounted in the kitchenette just inside an archway of his home. He was keeping an eye on Cates. The young punk tried to appear casual, leaning against the opposite wall of the kitchen.

Kelly stood nearby, paying close attention.

A strange contrast, thought McGavin, the taut tension here in his functional little kitchen of appliances, its small table for one and the bare essentials of dishes, utensils, pots and pans.

He said, "Colonel, the wrong people have this town wired. This is one boy we need to keep alive so he can tell us what he knows. I'll bring him in on my own when the time is right."

"And when will that be?"

Displeasure was obvious in the colonel's voice.

McGavin said, "I told Cates we'd accommodate whatever he wants within reason if he cooperates. What he wants is a face-to-face with the AG. That sounds reasonable to me."

"Sounds like a tall order for a piss-ant deserter."

"Under normal circumstances, yeah," McGavin agreed. "Not this time. Sir, I need you to fast-track this for us. This is about whatever Cho was investigating. I've got a hunch it all ties in. That's why the other side will try to shut it down if we give them the opportunity."

A brief pause ensued.

Then Ambrose said, "All right, I suppose that can be set up. But I know the ways of the Adjutant General, believe me. Best we'll be able to get Cates is first thing tomorrow morning."

"If that's the best we can do," said McGavin, "then okay. I'll babysit his worthless ass tonight."

"And you won't tell me where you are? You don't want backup?"

"What if your line's been tapped?"

"I doubt that, McGavin."

"You think it's an impossibility?"

"Well, I suppose it could be done. But our security—"

"I don't need help babysitting this little twerp," McGavin told him. "He'll be there first thing in the morning if you can set it up."

"Hold the line," said Ambrose. "I'll see what I can do."

A stretch of dead air across the line told McGavin he'd been put on hold. He never took his eyes from Cates. The punk slouched indolently against the wall.

Kelly asked McGavin, "Is everything okay?"

Cates smirked. "More than okay, sweet stuff," he said. "Your boyfriend's making it happen just like I told him to."

The hollow-sounding bravado got him a dirty look from McGavin who said, "Shut up, dipshit."

Cates closed his mouth, his cold eyes hooded and calculating.

The next couple of minutes took a long time. Then Ambrose clicked back on the line.

"All right, I've set it up. Tried for today but the AG's already left to attend some ceremony for the Viet President. I've been promised a full contingent bodyguard will be at his office waiting for you and Cates tomorrow morning at 0700. Be there, McGavin, and you'd better have that punk with you."

"I will. See you then, Colonel."

"At least tell me where you are," said Ambrose. "There's a helluva lot at stake here. I don't like it all riding on just your say-so."

"We've already discussed that, sir."

"We've also discussed you cutting back on this lone wolf cowboy shit."

"Colonel, this city has eyes and ears everywhere. The Vietcong have hit teams stashed throughout the city, ready to activate at a moment's notice with just a phone call. You and I know that's true. One of those teams would be glad to take us on in a street fight if they had to. I don't want to give them the opportunity. They could tumble to this deal anyway. If so, I'll take my chances but I don't want undue attention drawn here and that's all a backup unit would accomplish in my quiet neighborhood."

"McGavin, dammit—"

"The AG's office," said McGavin. "0700," and he hung up.

Cates couldn't stop smirking.

"Good work, Major." He jerked his head at Kelly, licking his lips with a lewd wink. "Who gets the whore, or do we share?"

"Shut it," said McGavin, "or I'll shut it for you."

Then he momentarily risked shifting his attention, parting a curtain a fraction of an inch to peer from the kitchen's single window out into the gathering dusk, checking for any indication that his address might under surveillance. He shifted his gaze from Cates for the briefest instant, thinking he could afford to since Cates at least knew he would be safe for tonight.

It had been a long day. Too long!

The brief moment checking the street outside was the opportunity Cates had been waiting for. The punk calculated his chances in that brief instant and went for it. Moving fast as a lightning bolt, he snatched up a chair at the small kitchen table. Using both hands to swing it around, he struck McGavin with the chair full-force across the back.

Catching McGavin by surprise, the blow slammed him to the wall beside the window. He hit a crouch instinctually as he pivoted, his right hand starting for the shoulder holstered .45. Cates continued moving lightning-fast. He tossed the chair aside, and when McGavin paused in his crouch with Cates in sight, the punk had already grabbed a nearby steak knife.

He had positioned himself behind Kelly, holding her before him as a human shield. His left forearm choked her against him while his right hand pressed the steak knife against her jugular vein. Kelly's eyes were wide, not with fear but with shock and pain at being manhandled.

McGavin froze, his fingers inches from the .45's butt. A chill coursed through him. His heartbeat seemed to catch in his throat.

Cates said, "The piece, Major. Take it out with your fingertips. Set it down on the floor and step back. Way back." He brought Kelly flush against him with a sharp, violent tug. "Do it and I won't off this bitch. Do it *now!*"

The knife's blade glinted against Kelly's throat. She said nothing, trusting McGavin who slowly and carefully drew the pistol from its holster, using his fingertips, and set the gun down upon the floor. Then he took several steps backward into the kitchen.

Cates pushed Kelly forcefully away from him. She almost lost her balance, but McGavin took a half-step forward and caught her in his arms, steadying her while Cates flung aside the knife, scooping up the .45 and flicking off its safety. He stepped away from them, reaching behind to unlatch the front street door, never taking his aim from where McGavin and Kelly stood together.

McGavin said, "Think about it, Specialist. You're in deep enough shit as it is. But maybe you're smart enough to live on the dodge and make it back to the World. You pull that trigger now and they'll hunt you down, no matter where you hide, and you'll go to hell facing a firing squad. Am I worth that?"

Cates considered that for a second, then he dashed out through the front doorway. Once outside his footfalls echoed loudly with his hasty withdrawal.

Kelly emitted a sigh of relief. She massaged where the blade had touched her jugular.

"Oh, Cord. I'm so sorry. I was standing too close to him—"

"Forget it," said McGavin, "I'm glad you're okay. Stay here. I'll be right back."

Retrieving a snubnosed .38 revolver that he always kept under a cushion of his reading chair, he stormed out in hot pursuit.

Chapter 14

....

McGavin burst onto the street.

Dusk was lengthening the shadows. Moderate foot traffic populated the sidewalks. Sparse vehicular traffic passed by. In the humid lethargy of the tail-end of this workday, the frantic running figure of Cates was easy to spot. The deserter was hauling ass, already halfway down the block, only seconds away from disappearing around the next street corner.

Cates suddenly stopped running, a subliminal impulse alerting him to danger. He whirled about, tracking McGavin's own .45 on McGavin.

McGavin raised his .38 in two-handed target acquisition, drawing a bead. It would not be an easy shot. He must place it well. Take the guy down. Disable Cates but don't kill him. Right now, the punk was his only lead.

Bystanders scattered. Frightened shouts filled the air.

Before Cates could fire, the scream of squealing tires shrieked, a maroon sedan of indeterminate age braked to an abrupt stop in the middle of the street. Its back doors flew open and a pair of gunmen burst from the car, each armed with a submachine gun. The first guy out triggered a sustained burst that riddled Cates, sending the deserter into a weird, shimmying boogie dance of death before his lifeless body crumpled to the pavement.

The second VC gunman needed an extra second or three to round the rear of the car, positioning himself for his shot at McGavin. Those vital seconds cost the guy his life. McGavin dropped to one knee and fired. No fancy shooting required this time. He squeezed off a quick one-two-three from his .38. The gunman caught each round in his chest, took a few stumbling steps and dropped dead.

The other gunman was leveling his weapon at Mc-Gavin, who automatically dodged to the side at the same instant the gunman opened fire. Staying low, McGavin scrambled across the distance toward the fallen body of Cates. The gunman continued triggering a sustained, sweeping burst, dozens of rounds attempting to catch up with McGavin but only shattering glass and riddling cars parked along the curb.

A break in the gunfire came as the VC triggerman hurriedly inserted a fresh magazine into his smoking weapon, allowing McGavin to gain the sprawled corpse just before the machine-gun fire resumed. Using the dead man for cover, McGavin slid the .38 under his belt. He grasped his .45 from the corpse's limp fingers. The bigger piece had more stopping power. The gunman's next burst of auto fire sent bullets spitting close over his head, also slapping into Cates's body. The corpse shuddered with the impact of each slug.

McGavin returned fire with his .45. Both his rounds caught the gunman in the chest, pitching him against the sedan. The weapon in his hands clattered to the pavement, and he followed it in a face-first fall.

That was enough for the sedan's driver, who goosed his gas pedal. The maroon sedan tore off away from the sprawl of bodies, picking up speed as it barreled toward the corner.

McGavin dashed into the middle of the street, clearing away from pedestrians and onlookers, angry at himself for having let Cates get away from him in the first place, thus causing this entire situation to spin out of control. He slammed off rounds after the sedan.

The sedan took fire and went into a wild wobble, the driver apparently hit. The out-of-control vehicle jumped the sidewalk without slowing. People scrambled in every direction for safety. The car plowed into the brick wall of a corner business with enough impact to shatter glass and crumple metal, the smash-up noise loud enough to carry all the way up the street. Then came the explosion, a *whoosh!* of an angry flash and the sedan was consumed by a raging eruption of smoke and fire.

The driver might have talked, if she'd survived, but no one could have survived a crash like that. Onlookers were cautiously approaching the crackling mass of flames that had been an automobile while McGavin turned and hustled back to his house, retrieving the jammed .38 along the way. The submachine guns, dropped by the dead gunmen, had already been filched by someone among the crowd of onlookers. Saigon was that sort of town.

But for now, the shooting seemed to be over. McGavin re-entered his home.

It was empty.

No sign of Kelly.

The sound of a vehicle accelerating hastily away from the alley behind the house!

McGavin ran through his house to the rear door beyond the kitchen. The back door loomed open. With the .45 held up and ready, he cautiously glanced around the doorframe, scanning the alley.

The alley held nothing but the shadows of dusk and its usual foul smells.

This had been a two-prong ambush intended to take out Cates *and* McGavin, who now processed it quickly in his mind. Two shooters on the street backed by a second hit team closing in from the alley. While Cates was buying the farm and McGavin was canceling the team out front, backup saw it go down and decided not to press their luck.

The second VC hit team was long gone.

And they'd taken Kelly with them . . .

* * *

Naturally, Kelly had no intention of obediently and politely sitting by and waiting when she'd been left behind in McGavin's house while he went out to pursue Cates. That was hardly her style, nor was it why she'd come to Vietnam.

She'd taken her camera from its bag and had started out the front door after McGavin. That's when the two Viet civilian guys came storming in through the back entrance holding submachine guns. When they saw Kelly, they shoulder-slung their weapons and were upon her.

It happened so fast. She tried to struggle but the two young males easily overpowered and physically restrained her. They rushed her through the house and out into the alley. She heard gunfire from in front of the house.

She was roughly tossed into the back seat of a parked Renault with a driver waiting. The two men followed her into the back seat. The doors slammed shut. The driver punched the accelerator. The car leaped away from there, up the alley and then turned onto the well-traveled cross-street. The Renault merged with the traffic flow.

The whole incident had taken no more than two or three minutes.

Kelly twisted in the confines of the back seat, addressing the men crowding her on either side in Vietnamese.

"Who are you? Let me out of here! Let me—"

The one on her right, whose name was Chuong, punched her sharply on the jaw.

Kelly's eyes rolled back in their sockets. She crumpled into the narrow space on the floor.

The Renault tooled along. It was hot and stuffy in the car. The driver chuckled from behind the steering wheel.

"She has spirit, this one!"

Chuong gazed down at the unconscious woman. He massaged his knuckles.

He said, "It will not be easy for her."

"I know," said the driver. "If you want to know the truth, I feel sorry for her."

Chapter 15

....

The surprised look in Major Cho's eyes clearly indicated that the last person he expected to see walking into his office was Cord McGavin. He rose from behind his desk with cold professionalism.

It was less than an hour since the shooting of Cates and the abduction of Kelly.

McGavin hardly expected a cordial greeting from his ARVN counterpart. His ID had brought him through the layers of perimeter security at the ARVN central HQ complex. Cho's CID unit was easy enough to locate.

McGavin tried to break the ice with, "Working late, eh? An honest soldier's work is never done."

Cho said, "We have nothing to discuss, McGavin. Why are you here?"

"I'm here to cut through the bullshit," said McGavin.

"It's time for us to level with each other, Cho. Time for us to pool what we have and see what can get done."

"Indeed?"

"Yeah, indeed. Let's start with, Why the hell are you so damn pissed off and bent out of shape about that shootout on the docks? Damn, guy, me showing up down there saved your ass."

"That is conjecture."

"American servicemen were involved," McGavin pressed. "That's not conjecture. That's fact. Dead GIs in body bags. That makes it my business, in addition to the fact that I'm the one who took them down. So how about we talk?"

Cho remained standing.

"I spoke on the telephone with Colonel Ambrose a short while ago, requesting an update on your status among other things. He told me you've apprehended a deserter."

"Cates," McGavin confirmed with a nod. "A lot has happened in that short while since you and the colonel spoke and I'm here to tell you about it. Cates is dead. A VC hit team nailed him before I took them down."

Cho said, "Unfortunate."

"Yeah, you do have the gift for understatement, Major. I don't know how they honed in on us but they did and it was a bloody mess. I came straight here from the scene."

"After reporting to Colonel Ambrose what happened, of course."

"Negative," said McGavin. "I'm tired of getting bullshit everywhere I turn on this deal. That's why I'm here."

A frown wrinkled Cho's brow.

"The colonel is unaware that you're here?"

"Far as I know."

"Why?"

"Let's get back to my question first," said McGavin. "I want a real conversation, Cho. A back and forth. And it's your turn. Why were you so pissed about me saving your life? And if it was heavy enough for those punks to try and wipe you out, why wasn't I brought into the loop before that? You and I have worked together to our mutual advantage. Why not this time?"

Cho reached a decision. His demeanor warmed but only somewhat. He sat behind his desk and motioned to one of the two visitor chairs. McGavin sat but he could not relax. He leaned forward, unable to contain the intensity of his emotion.

Cho said, "You did perform nobly in my best interest, that is true. However, I was and still am displeased by your presence there. You and Colonel Ambrose were not confided in because I have come to suspect that a high-level American officer is involved in what I'm investigating. I make no excuses. I do not know who to trust on your side and so I trust no one."

"I need you to trust me," said McGavin. "I need information that only you can provide. And for me, this one's personal."

Cho considered this.

Then he said, "Very well. I will trust you, McGavin. You did save my life. And frankly, I could well benefit from the trust of someone in your camp. That has not been easy to come by in light of your group having an informant among my personnel."

"Wasn't my idea," McGavin assured him, "and I'm not the one who set it up. Have you confronted the spy in your ranks?"

"It is too late for that," said Cho. "A young woman in our typist pool. A troubled young woman, apparently. She died of a drug overdose this afternoon. It is too early to tell if it was accidental or suicide, according to our medical examiner."

"And according to you?"

Cho registered a mild shrug.

"I was a police officer here in Saigon before this war began. A homicide investigator. Someone is back-tracking. Covering their tracks. Is that the appropriate analogy?"

"It'll do. Colonel Ambrose is the one who made her an asset. But you know that."

Cho nodded. "When I spoke to the colonel about you, I also asked if he knew anything about her death. Ambrose claimed to not even know she was dead."

McGavin said, "Huh."

Cho studied McGavin thoughtfully.

"You and I come from different worlds," he said. "Or at least from different cultures. There are few, if any, points where our backgrounds are similar. And yet here we are, two ex-police officers brought together because of war. Now our lives intersect and we must work together. This I accept because, American, I sense that as men we may be very much alike. But what arrogance makes you think that this is not also highly personal for me?"

McGavin could not take his mind from Kelly. What fate could be hers as he sat here conversing with this guy? He wanted whatever information Cho could supply and then to push on at full-tilt to get his wife back before it was too late. But he knew a breakthrough when he saw one . . .

"I meant no offense, Cho. It's why we work well together. It's why I took this man-to-man approach with you now."

Cho's features were unreadable when he said, "My daughter died earlier this year from a drug overdose."

The softly-spoken comment caught McGavin by surprise, blindsiding his runaway emotions.

He said, "I'm sorry."

"She was living with us while she attended the university. Her grades were very good at first. But she began to socialize with the wrong people and, soon, my wife and I noticed changes in her. Her grades went down. She missed classes. Stayed out late hours and sometimes did not come home until morning. We confronted her about this and it never ended well. And now she is dead. A bright child with a bright future. Gone forever." The only change in Cho as he spoke was a tightening of his hands into fists upon his desktop. "Nothing about this war is good for my country. Was it General Grant in your American civil war who said, "War is hell?" The young especially turn to hard drugs in increasing numbers to numb their fears and anxieties. A tragic situation. While warfare tears my country apart, the horrific toll of life taken yearly by the insidious trafficking of drugs is truly beyond belief."

McGavin's personal opinion of the man increased tenfold. Every word he spoke was the truth. Vietnam was a major transit country for drug traffickers moving heroin from the Golden Triangle area of Laos and Burma to markets in the West. The growing indication of a GI heroin addiction epidemic in Vietnam was another result and a serious concern.

Cho continued, "And so, now you know why this case matters to me. It's an investigation I've initiated on and off duty. Your GIs tried to ambush me on the waterfront with the help of a drug dealer I was there to meet. They know I'm getting close. My daughter cries out from beyond for justice."

McGavin said, "This drug thing will only get worse. It's got to be shut down fast."

Cho's eyes narrowed. He studied McGavin anew.

"And what of you, McGavin? You tell me your deserter is dead. Unfortunate, but in war men die every day. You and I must perform our duties as the professionals we are, no more, no less. Yet you forgo reporting the deserter's death and you come to me instead, requesting my help because for you this is now a personal matter. So tell me, McGavin, *why* is this now personal for you?"

Their conversation reminded McGavin of shifting sands. In his mind, Kelly's elaborate deception to get herself into his world had evaporated. The only constant remained the urgency of locating and rescuing her. Cho had been an adversary when McGavin walked into this office. Now the vital help he needed depended on convincing Cho exactly how much that help was needed and exactly how much it mattered to him as a man. Shifting sands, yeah.

"They have my wife," said McGavin. "It's a long story and I won't take up time with it now. But whoever ordered the hit on Cates has kidnapped my wife. Simple as that."

Cho was sharp as a tack but anyone would have trouble swallowing that one. He blinked.

"She's here in Vietnam? Your wife?"

"It wasn't my doing," McGavin assured him, "but that's what I'm dealing with. They'll lure me into a trap using her."

"Has anyone contacted you?"

"Not yet. I haven't given them the opportunity. Cho, I've *got* to find her. I *will* find her. I'll move heaven and earth. I'll blitz into Hell itself if I have to. That's why I'm going vigilante. It's why I need whatever information you can supply me with that could possibly concern her whereabouts. Can you help me?

Cho spoke without hesitation.

"Here's what I know from my personal investigation. It may help you. A drug pipeline direct from the Golden Triangle is being set up by American soldiers who intend to ship hard drugs back to the United States on a regular basis for distribution."

"Cates and that crew on the dock were part of that?"

"They did the dirty work," said Cho with a nod. "But there is someone higher up the chain of command who has put the organization for it together. I hesitate to say this but that someone could be your superior, Colonel Ambrose."

McGavin said with a sigh, "I hope not. I sort of like the colonel."

"It is only conjecture at this point."

McGavin's mind was clicking into overdrive.

"VC hit teams are positioned throughout the city to be dispatched at a moment's notice. The colonel put me on hold on the telephone while he claimed to be contacting the Adjutant General a short time before a team hit my place and I'd told no one where we were. The timing is right if a VC team was nearby and, if that's the case, it sure as hell would establish a tie-in between the Vietcong, Ambrose and your Golden Triangle drug peddlers."

"When it comes to drug profits," said Cho, "the dealers' only allegiance is to the payoff. A big deal is scheduled to go down tonight if my information is correct. I have been helpless to move against it since I have no one to trust . . . until now."

"Tell me about this big deal."

"The man I suspect of putting this together is Dinh Quang. He was a ranking politician in our government before being pressured out due to his leftist leanings. He owns an estate in the suburbs and is well-insulated thanks to bribery and a paramilitary security force said to include a Vietcong element."

"And he can't be touched?"

"He cannot. Not legally. We placed two undercover agents within his operation during the last six months; both disappeared and were never heard from again. But the operation is big enough for word to filter down to street level now and then."

"Rumblings," said McGavin.

"A suitable term for what I mean, yes," nodded Cho. "Rumblings. Not hard facts that will produce warrants in a corrupt system. But when you hear those rumblings in the stormy sky, they are real and they speak of a real storm about to break. Enough of these rumblings have been put together in my investigation and indicate that Dinh will be receiving a major shipment of heroin from Laos. The whispered word on the street—the rumblings—indicate it has been arranged this very night for Dinh to receive the heroin shipment at his estate where he will transfer it to the American servicemen he's aligned with."

"And how are they planning to smuggle the heroin out of Vietnam?"

"Body bags."

"Body bags?"

"An ingenious plan, wouldn't you say? Who would ever suspect such a means of shipment? Accomplices have been embedded stateside at the other end of this new pipeline. When the bodies arrive there for processing before being turned over to the next of kin, the heroin will be removed from the body bags before the remains are transferred."

"That's obscene." The words came out in a low, hoarse whisper that McGavin barely recognized as his own voice. "And this ties in with Kelly?"

"Kelly? Your wife?"

McGavin nodded. He said nothing.

Cho continued, "Dinh is the power behind the Viet side of this equation. It is highly likely that the American officer who has joined in this foul scheme will also be present tonight at Dinh's estate. If your wife is not being held there, someone there will know where she is being held. But legally, I don't see how—" He ended the thought with another shrug of resignation.

"Legally," McGavin repeated. "You keep using that word. But it wasn't a legal, officially sanctioned investigation that brought you down to that waterfront pier, was it? It was those rumblings. And I wasn't down there legally because of orders. I was there because I heard the rumblings too. I'm operating off the record, just like you are. What does that tell you, Cho?"

Cho considered McGavin with his unreadable eyes.

"What should it tell me, my friend?"

McGavin arched an eyebrow. "Friend?"

"Yes, friend. Tell me what you wish to say."

"I don't have to tell you," said McGavin. "You already know. You just have to tell me, Are you in or out? I'm hitting that estate tonight and, if they are holding Kelly, I'm liable to level the damn place. I've got a friendly armorer who can supply everything I need. So, you tell me, friend Cho. We were both down on the waterfront on our own initiative. Your daughter and my wife make this personal with both of us. What do you say?"

Cho registered a slight smile. "I say . . . what is it you have in mind?"

Chapter 16

....

When the BMW limousine reached the crest of the hill, Colonel Ambrose leaned forward and spoke to his Vietnamese driver.

"Slow here for a moment. I want to look."

"Yes, sir."

The powerful car slowed to coasting speed down the hill and into the valley where Dinh Quang had his estate.

It was one of the old rubber plantations that had never recovered its feet after World War II; instead, it had become a residence for the very wealthy. The valley of estates below this crest of the hill was bathed in moonlight, creating a patchwork pattern for a considerable distance.

Ambrose wore pressed military khaki even though he was off duty. A uniform and his rank would surely command respect and that always made things easier. Much had gone into the planning of this enterprise he had undertaken. He was "sleeping with the enemy" but the stakes were worth it. After a lifetime of service to his country and all it stood for and now, with his retirement approaching, it was *his* turn. He would make the big financial kill that would set him up for the rest of his life in comfort and luxury, a fair exchange for a lifetime of loyal duty and tonight was the starting point that would set the whole future of his life in motion.

He focused his attention on a thorough study of what he could make out of Dinh Quang's estate. The ex-senator had done rather well for himself, his Marxist rhetoric notwithstanding.

What appeared from this distance to be ten-foot-high stone walls surrounded the fifteen-acre parcel of real estate. The main entrance to the grounds was a heavy metal gate bolted into the wall. Within the walls, tapered lawns and well-maintained shrubbery and a forest of trees lent the place a tranquil, pastoral elegance.

The main house, limned in silver by the moon's illumination, was a three-level affair. There were a few outbuildings and one extended garage. In the dim illumination of a single outdoor light, a helicopter sat on a landing pad behind the house—a light, bubble-front two-seater with civilian markings. It was the type that would ferry a millionaire businessman here and there about the city. The garage held an armored urban assault vehicle. Dinh had previously bragged to Ambrose that he employed a top-flight mercenary security force of more than a dozen men from both the Vietcong *and* the ARVN.

Clouds blotted out the moon, shrouding the estate in darkness except for the isolated circle of light around the helicopter.

Ambrose had utilized his considerable CID resources to deep-profile the big fish architect of this operation only to learn that Dinh's political and criminal activities were effectively obscured behind a front of legitimate bureaucratic complexity and systemic corruption dating back to the senator's days in office.

Ambrose leaned forward again and said to the driver, "I've seen enough. Continue on."

"Yes, sir."

The sleek car picked up speed with no more than the purring of a contented kitten.

It had been easy enough, once he left CID HQ, for Colonel Ambrose to put walking distance between himself and the American base, making certain he was not being tailed before casually boarding the BMW that drew up on a busy side street at exactly the pre-arranged time.

There was no reason anyone should suspect him of anything, Ambrose assured himself. After a lifetime of military service, his record was spotless. He'd been a good soldier for his entire adult life and, with his retirement rapidly approaching, no one expected him to be anything else.

He thought about Dinh Quang, his recently-acquired partner in crime. Once he'd decided to somehow find and pursue an extralegal path in building his personal retirement fund, as commanding officer of a CID detachment, he'd begun keeping an eye open for some contact point to begin manifesting what he had in mind. He'd found what he was looking for in the nowhere case file of an E-2 caught selling reefer on post. The kid got the reefer from an ARVN guy and, after he had followed that chain, who should contact the colonel but Dinh himself?

Ambrose had at first been cautious in the extreme, in case it was some sort of green machine sting. He pretended to act doubtful about this plan Dinh proposed. But inside he knew this was *it*. He could not see how Dinh's scheme could fail.

The fly in the ointment was that damn McGavin, who'd managed to evade the hit teams sent to grease him and Cates. But with that woman, Kelly Carpenter, now held hostage at Dinh's estate, it would be simple enough to transport her someplace where McGavin could be drawn into a vain rescue attempt that would end in his and the woman's death.

And in the meantime?

A carnal heat stirred within Ambrose. He knew it was not healthy but this only excited him more. That Carpenter bitch was a good-looking piece of work, damn straight. A mental image came to him of the woman bound, stripped and helpless . . . *at his mercy!* It was very exciting to think about. He wondered what else this night would hold beyond the start of a new adventure . . .

A warm drizzling mist began as the BMW reached the bottom of the hill. At the front gate of Dinh's estate, the driver braked for inspection by the posted sentries who wore the uniforms of security personnel. One of the sentries strode over to the car.

Ambrose nodded approvingly to himself. The sentries surely recognized the car and the license plates by now but the side windows of the BMW were smoked glass and so this sentry was advancing to make sure while his partner covered the car from inside the gate with a rifle. Ambrose fingered the mechanism for lowering the window.

The sentry stared in briefly. Then he straightened in a hurry and nodded to the man inside the gate. The iron gate yawned open. The BMW purred on through. Ambrose closed the window and relaxed back against the plush interior. They gained speed along the slight incline toward the house.

Dinh stood waiting for him beneath the portico, a lithe, fiftyish man who appeared aloof. His eyes, as always, were concealed behind the reflecting sunglasses he habitually wore even on a rainy evening like this.

The BMW coasted to a stop. Dinh watched as the chauffeur climbed out from behind the wheel and hurried back to open the rear door for Ambrose, who emerged holding a thin leather briefcase.

Dinh said, "Welcome to my home, Colonel. I trust you had a pleasant drive out from the city."

He turned without awaiting a response and led the way into the house.

Ambrose found himself hurrying to keep up. Those sunglasses Dinh wore always had an unsettling effect on him which he was now trying to ignore. For the last several nights, he would have been unable to sleep had it not been for the massive doses of sedatives prescribed by his physician. Yet, even through the day-after grogginess, he could still feel the quivering in his stomach lining that would not stop.

He had come to realize at this point in his life that his real talent lay in deception, in the subtleties of politics and secrecy. He was no longer a frontline-ready fighting man. That was a lifetime ago. Everything in his life these days was directing him toward making this big kill before he cut it all loose for a well-banked retirement.

But he never felt comfortable around Dinh . . .

Chapter 17

....

For something to say, Ambrose said, "I appreciate you sending the ride in to pick me up. I'm getting to like the good life."

He immediately regretted the triteness of the remark.

Dinh made no reply. He led Ambrose down a first-floor hallway. Members of his security force, in uniform, were about the house. An air of preparation and anticipation prevailed.

The private library was dominated by an immense oak desk. The wall behind the desk was artfully decorated with certificates, awards and a pre-war photograph of the senator shaking hands with the Vietnamese president. Below that was a cabinet containing what looked like TV monitors, their screens currently dark. Two walls of the room were lined floor to ceiling with leather-bound volumes. A few wingchairs were drawn up near the desk and a few healthy potted plants rested here and there. Rain pattered gently outside a screen door that led out to a patio.

Ambrose said, "I, uh, trust this rain will not . . . interfere with our business tonight, senator."

"It need hardly concern us," Dinh replied. He eyed the briefcase. "You have brought the information I requested?"

Ambrose nodded, grateful the man was all business with no interest in trading idle chitchat. He tapped the briefcase with an index finger and set the briefcase on the desk.

"Right here and a lot of work went into it, believe me."

"Very good, Colonel. It is with considerable satisfaction and anticipation that I look forward to turning America into a nation of drug addicts. In addition to the profit incentive, it is a mission Hanoi and our masters in China will no doubt find most inspired . . . and inspiring."

Ambrose did his best not to display the revulsion he felt at such talk, another reason for his heavy use of sedatives. But he reminded himself that it would only be negroes and the other criminal classes who would be using the heroin. Why should he care about them? Didn't every community in America employ a police force to protect their city from drug users and criminals? This is simply too perfect a deal to pass by, he told himself yet again.

And there was that carnal heat lingering from his erotic thoughts about Kelly Carpenter . . .

"Uh, what about the woman?" he asked. "Is she here? Are you holding her?"

"Serendipitous, is it not?" Dinh said. "The man, McGavin, escapes my men alive and yet we now have his woman."

"I'm not sure she's *his* woman," said Ambrose. "I only know he has feelings and a sense of responsibility for her, being the kind of man he is. She's the key to trapping him. But Dinh, about the woman . . . uh, may I see her?"

Dinh's eyes held a glimmer of amusement, here and gone.

"And why would you want to see her, may I ask?"

"Come on, senator." Ambrose forced himself to send the man a wink. "We're both men of the world. She's a beautiful young lady, wouldn't you say?"

"She is that."

"Well, I guess I just want to look in on the lady and, er, see how she's doing, let's say."

Dinh said, "Ah."

"She *is* here, right? Your team brought her here as I suggested?"

"I do not follow the suggestions of a traitor," Dinh said mildly. "It is to *my* advantage, Colonel, to eliminate this man McGavin if he indeed poses a threat too."

"As long as we put him down," said Ambrose. "I hate to do it because, well, he's such a damn good investigator. But we have no choice, do we?"

"We do not."

"I assigned him to locate the deserter, Cates, because we wanted them both out of the way and why not use one of your VC teams to do it? But it bothers me that Mc-Gavin dropped out of sight. I should have heard from him after he walked away from that hit on his home. He sure as hell poses a threat. We've got to move fast to nail his ass."

Dinh said, "I feel the same way about Major Cho of the ARVN." He indicated the briefcase. "Open it," he ordered. "I wish to see what you brought me."

With his right thumb, Ambrose clicked the combination, unlocking the briefcase. He withdrew a manila folder and handed it to Dinh, who glanced over a typed list on a single sheet of paper within. Ambrose re-latched the briefcase, setting it at his feet. Dinh looked up from the page with a satisfied nod.

"You have served me well."

"I haven't served anyone but my government," Ambrose replied somewhat stiffly, "and I'm here serving my own damn self. This is our *joint* endeavor, right, senator? You and me are setting up a gravy train that will keep on running for as long as this war goes on."

"Quite right," Dinh said in his mild, slightly bemused voice that was starting to grate on Ambrose's nerves.

Dinh quite knew the effect his manner was having on his guest. This was his intention though, honestly, he could hardly care less considering what was about to happen.

His life had been an eventful one and had taken him a long, long way from his humble peasant beginnings. Along the way, he'd let nothing interfere in a quest for prestige and power that could only be born of earthy poverty and relentless ambition.

Born in Phan Rang on the South Central Coast of Vietnam forty years earlier, as a young man, Dinh had flirted with communism. It was everywhere in Southeast Asia following the war. He'd left Phan Rang as a teenager, never to return, but not before forming alliances among the communist cohorts that proved most beneficial years later.

Joining the occupying French-backed military, he'd risen through the ranks and, when the French withdrew and the ARVN came into existence, Dinh headed the Vietnamese National Military Academy before becoming a division commander and colonel. As part of the military coalition that staged a coup, toppling the ruling government in 1963, Dinh had become a general, navigating several short-lived juntas and seizing yet more power by adopting a cautious approach while other officers around him defeated and sidelined each another.

When he branched into the private sector, into politics, ever increasing his off-shore bank accounts, his prestige and power continued to grow. He consolidated the disparate political and military forces loose in his country, ultimately commanding a power base that had brought him to his present pinnacle of power. Dinh had not accomplished any of this by suffering fools gladly.

Ambrose was saying, "So how about it, Dinh? You've got what you want. That's the list of names and means of contact for all the servicemen we've paid off stateside to handle transferring the contraband from the body bags to the civilians waiting to distribute. They are the middlemen in other words, the final link in the chain I've put together." He nodded at the dark monitors against the wall. "So now how's about doing a little favor for me? I'd sure like a look at that woman your boys brought home from McGavin's place. I'm betting you've got a short circuit TV camera trained on her right now."

"And you only wish to look?"

Ambrose smirked and realized he was licking his lips.

"I'd want some time alone to use her," he said. "Wouldn't you, Dinh? Hell yeah and damn straight. I want to have my way with that haughty bitch. I want to—"

Dinh wrinkled his nose with distaste. "Enough." He

flicked a button on the monitor console. One of the screens lit up.

And there she was!

Ambrose felt his heartbeat increase. His throat grew dry. His dick started getting hard. Even with the unease he felt in having to deal with Dinh and his damn reflector shades, the heat in his groin spread pleasurably throughout his body at the very sight of her. The small monitor left nothing to the imagination.

She was tied to a plain wooden kitchen chair, her ankles bound to the chair legs with a plasticized clothesline, her wrists similarly bound behind her. When her image appeared, she was straining against her bonds.

Ambrose found her gyrations erotic, the way her clothes strained tightly against her supple figure, the movement of her breasts and torso. He'd wanted her sexually since the moment she and McGavin had walked into his office at CID headquarters. She was tied to a chair now somewhere in this very house!

Dinh's mild voice interrupted his overheated, racing thoughts.

"My man, Chuong, has been guarding her. You see, he is the boss of the crew that found her. They brought her here and so I have promised Chuong that after Miss Carpenter has served her purpose, he may have her before she is done away with."

Ambrose felt his smirk grow wider. He licked his lips again. Perspiration was beading across his receding hairline. He was on the verge of yielding to obsession. *Perhaps I already have*, he told himself. But the sight of the bound woman on the monitor screen was arousing him beyond reason. *I've already sold my soul to the Devil! Here's my chance to indulge my darkest appetite!* Ambrose could not take his eyes off that monitor.

He heard himself say, "Hell, Dinh, I don't mind sloppy seconds. Your boy did the heavy lifting so, okay, he can have her first. But come on. She'll be useless and dead soon as we get McGavin. Let me have her just once." Ambrose indicated the manila folder. "You've got what you want."

"That is so," nodded Dinh, "and that being the case, Colonel, surely you can appreciate why I now no longer have need of you. The soldiers on this list in the United States and here in-country work for *me* now. My people have already set this in motion."

Ambrose brought his attention from the monitor, scowling.

"What the hell are you talking about?"

In response, Dinh merely gazed over the colonel's shoulder at something behind Ambrose. He nodded.

Ambrose started to turn.

Chuong swooped in from behind, wrapping each end of the garrote in a fist and lowering it around the colonel's throat. He had slipped silently into the library, his presence undetected by Ambrose . . . until now.

He began to strangle Ambrose, who commenced dancing a frantic jig against him, his fingers clawing desperately at the garrote, gasping in vain for air. Then, gradually, the harsh wheezing tapered off. His struggles weakened. When the tattoo of shoe heels upon the floor finally stopped, Chuong applied more effort for an additional minute to make certain. He lowered Ambrose to the floor, unwinding the garrote from around the throat. His nostrils twitched at the stench of the dead man's voided bowels. He straightened from his task.

Dinh said, "Well done, Chuong. See that this garbage is removed. Then return to guarding our prisoner."

"Yes, senator. At once."

Chuong stepped to the library doorway. He drew the door open, about to summon men from his crew to perform the task. He heard something unusual. It took him a second to identify what he was hearing.

Senator Dinh was urinating on the corpse.

Upon completing this act, the senator said, "Always bear in mind, Chuong, that there is nothing lower in life than a traitor."

Chapter 18

....

After being knocked unconscious in the Renault, Kelly regained consciousness with a gasp that stayed trapped in her throat because electrical tape had been pasted across her mouth. The gasp almost choked her it was so strong, born of pain racing through her and the panic that came from being unable to see.

She was blindfolded!

She came instantly alert, aware of her situation. Her pain emanated from soreness in her jaw, pulsating as if on fire. She managed to establish that she was bound to a low-backed chair. It was not comfortable. She thought, *thank God I'm in decent physical condition from all those gym workouts back home. And thank God I'm still wearing my clothes!*

She couldn't see but she could feel and hear. She felt

closeness. She was in a small room. The air was warm. She detected her own scent and she was glad she was wearing perfume. And close by . . . *someone was breathing*, a shallow, normal, steady breathing, not excited or lascivious but constant and nerve-wracking.

It took a few moments more for her to summon the final events before she'd lost consciousness, like waking and trying to recall your final thoughts before you fell asleep the night before. Then she recalled the sudden explosion of violence in Cord's home.

Sudden, yes.

In the movies and cheap fiction she'd been raised on, violence was a thing that happened following simmering suspense and a dramatic buildup like, say, the end of a movie or right before cutting to a commercial on TV. But it hadn't happened that way. Cord brought the deserter, Cates, to his residence for safekeeping and the explosion of violence flared with prelude when Cates made his break, ending with gunfire in the street and a sock to her jaw from the VC gunmen who had poured into Cord's house from the back alley.

And now, here she was.

Kelly's next thought came unbidden. Was Cord right? Her husband had hardly minced words in voicing his disapproval of her coming to Saigon. True, she'd covered street crime in America but this was war in a foreign land. Should she have stayed home? Did she really belong here? Who did she think she was, going wherever she felt like in a hostile, violent world of strangers?

She cast aside this moment of doubt with a silent, angry self-recrimination. She reminded herself that her place was wherever her heart took her.

Where was Cord now?

The gunfire in the street out in front of his house before she'd been abducted . . . surely he survived whatever skirmish his pursuit of Cates had drawn him into. Then it came to her that she was likely alive because her husband was alive. Cord wasn't dead. In Kelly's mind, the competent, rock-solid *maleness* of the man she loved was invincible. There weren't many guys around these days like Cord McGavin. She told herself, *I'm alive because I'm serving a purpose. They'll use me to trap Cord. They know he'll be coming for his woman.*

She should have done more to resist when those gunmen tossed her into the Renault. She was a self-reliant, in-shape woman, for crying out loud! She knew martial arts. She understood the strengths and weaknesses of the human body. She should have applied defensive force against those goons the instant they tried to grab her. *Stop it*, she told herself. Hindsight was always 20-20.

Martial arts were among the many things Cord McGavin had contributed to her life. The wrong turns that brought her challenges and obstacles she had mostly brought on herself, her current situation being a perfect example.

But it was not Kelly's nature to dwell on misfortune but, rather, to always keep her thoughts positive, directed toward higher ground and resolution. She told herself she would not die here, wherever the hell she was. She would see this through. She was a survivor. That's what she told herself and her affirmation came when her thoughts dwelled on the man to whom she'd given her heart.

Why does a woman love one particular man above all others?

She'd met Cord after noticing him at the gym. There

was just something about the way the man carried himself and the smooth, natural flow of his musculature as he worked out. Then he started showing up at the yoga sessions she'd enrolled in. By then her interest had been well-drawn.

He introduced himself after a yoga session. They spoke of the usual things at first. The gym. The weather. He suggested coffee and she did not hesitate to accept. Months later, after they'd become lovers and a couple, Cord confessed that she'd caught his interest as well, seeing her about the gym. It turned out he'd enrolled in the yoga class not only because he practiced yoga on his own but primarily because he'd wanted to meet her.

They spoke of the importance they each placed on maintaining a healthy *chi*, the circulating life energy that in Chinese philosophy is thought to be inherent in all things, the balance of negative and positive believed to be essential for the body's optimum health and function. By the time they said goodnight and agreed to see each other again, Kelly was sold.

While she'd never really mastered martial arts, the rudimentary moves Cord taught her came in handy on one occasion when a photojournalist assignment had placed her in a dicey situation with a cell of domestic terrorists. She'd embedded herself as an airhead wannabe and when they found out she was news media, two of those thugs got her alone, unsuspecting, and had actually tried to do her in. One held her from behind while the other had a sap he intended to use on her. He got kicked in the nuts instead while the guy holding her got his face busted up from a head butt, allowing Kelly to escape.

That happened months before she and Cord got married, so her future husband did know what he was getting himself into. Life is full of clichés when you're in love but their romance had never lost its luster. Even her mom and dad liked Cord! Those were the reasons she loved this particular man. She had a life worth holding onto and thinking about it helped to sustain the flicker of hope within her.

But there was no denying she was in one hell of a mess.

There was no way to keep track of time. There was only the utter darkness of being blindfolded, the aching muscles from having been bound to the chair for an extended period of time and the closeness and vague threat of another presence. She tired of working her wrists to loosen them from the plastic clothesline binding them. The pain told her she was only grinding away at flesh with no hope of loosening her bonds. Panic was a half-awake, concealed beast that lived inside her quivering stomach muscles, tightening and loosening and tightening again in spasms.

She took in long draws of air through her nostrils, twitching her mouth beneath the duct tape. She was completely, effectively gagged. All of the hassles that had troubled her—her passionate reunion with Cord despite his disapproval, the determination to persevere on this mission of hers no matter what—seemed almost trivial, insignificant now, tied to a chair God knows where, blindfolded, being studied by someone who had left her alone for a while before recently returning to resume his silent vigil over her with nothing between them but breathing and silence.

She must remain confident. Don't panic. She assured herself, again and again, *I will survive!* But by not breaking down and emotionally falling apart in front of this person in this close place, wherever they were.

Her captor's breathing was the only sound she heard. Sounded like a man. He lit a cigarette. The smoke made her cough.

And so, she lost track of how long she sat there. He smoked cigarettes nonstop, adding two new sounds to her dark world, the click of his lighter and the audible exhalation of his smoking. It could have been an hour; it could have been four hours.

She was incredibly thirsty.

At times, her heartbeat thundered in her ears and then she would talk herself into calming down. There were perverted sickos out there, war or no war, and Kelly hoped to God that she hadn't fallen into one of their hands.

Did Cord even know of her predicament?

What in the world would happen next?

Chapter 19

....

Cord and Cho crouched at a point above the northwest corner of the high brick wall that surrounded Senator Dinh's property. The countryside might have appeared pastoral and exclusive in the sunshine but, on this rainy night, the darkness of the elements matched what Mc-Gavin felt inside.

They wore jackets against the mist. A breeze had nipped in, giving the mist a bite. Beneath the jackets, each man wore his sidearm in a shoulder holster, and a military webbing of grenades, ammo, and penetration gear. The head weapon for each man on this hit was a silenced Ingram MAC Model 10 machine gun, a short, compact SMG chambered for .45 rounds in a 30-round magazine. The lightweight, diminutive MAC-10 was accurate enough for short-range outdoor firing and was a vicious "room broom" for close-in indoor action.

A blacktopped road twisted down from a rise to travel across the extended shelf of land that had been sectioned off into the private walled estates. There had been little traffic along the blacktop. McGavin had steered them past the front gate, traveling on a short distance, turning onto the inconspicuous, bumpy trail that led up to this position overlooking the old rubber plantations.

He'd parked the van so he and Cho could creep over to this overlook and get a clear look down onto much of Dinh's estate and the public road that ran past it. From this high ground concealment, they studied, with infrared binoculars, what they could see inside the estate walls.

A white panel van was drawing up to a stop next to a side entrance of the main house. The truck's tail lights remained on, indicating the driver was letting the engine idle. A man emerged from the van's passenger side and hurried around to open the van's rear doors. As if on cue, the side door of the building snapped inward. A pair of men emerged, carrying a body. The one being carried was unconscious or worse, supported under the shoulders by one man while the first, leading the way, held the body's ankles, one to his either side.

McGavin tightened the focus on his binoculars. He recognized the features of the man being carried.

"Damn," he said. "You were right, Cho. Ambrose is dirty as they come."

Cho said, "And the colonel seems not to be having a good time of it."

As they watched, the colonel's body was flung unceremoniously into the cargo hold of the van. It was not difficult to imagine the thump his body made and the body did not move or twitch.

The colonel was dead meat.

The killing had begun down there . . .

McGavin's gut tightened with apprehension. For him, only one thing mattered: finding Kelly and, if she was down there, getting her the hell out whatever the cost. He and Cho had been taking care of business with all the speed they could summon. But Ambrose's death meant time had already run out.

The last couple of hours had flown by on a fast track, cutting through red tape, calling in favors and bypassing paperwork on both the US and ARVN sides of the bureaucratic fence. McGavin's high estimation of Cho at the start of tonight's endeavor, when he'd offered Cho a piece of this action, was only continuing to rise minute by minute. They had functioned well together and, for sure, their individual m.o.'s were pretty much from the same rulebook which is to say they knew how to break every rule that needed breaking in order to bring the mission to its successful conclusion.

They'd spoken little to each other from the time they left Cho's office to this point on a rainy overlook in an upscale suburb of Saigon. McGavin could tell the guy was totally together by the way he performed—skillfully and tactfully negotiating protocol to get them what they needed from his resources. This had been a cooperative effort all the way.

Down below, the rear doors of the van were slammed shut. It looked very much like the routine work of three men who knew what they were doing. Everybody was hunching against the light rain. The pair from the building returned inside and the other boarded the passenger side of the van.

The driver backed the van around and drove down to the front gate, where the sentries had the gates open. The van sailed through, taking a right turn and following the public road away from the city, deeper into the impenetrable gloom of the rainy countryside.

Cho said, "I am willing to bet that is the last anyone will ever see of your Colonel Ambrose."

McGavin said, "Good riddance to bad trash."

"He could have supplied us with information," said Cho, "but, yes, justice has been served."

McGavin peered along the opposite direction of the road taken by the van.

"What's this?"

Cho swung his binoculars around to hone in on McGavin's line of vision.

An armored urban assault vehicle chugged down the rise behind them in the rain, descending the blacktop road toward their position, its diesel fumes polluting the atmosphere. On the vehicle's side was the insignia and ID numbering of the South Vietnamese Army. The vehicle passed the point where the highway curved well past and below their position, continuing on before braking at Dinh's front gate, which remained open from the exit of the white van.

A sentry ambled over to the ARVN vehicle and examined some papers the driver showed him. Then the assault vehicle drove out of McGavin and Cho's sight—their position was not high enough to see every part of the property inside those stone walls but it was the best vantage point they could find on short notice.

McGavin said, "You told me Dinh is well connected to

the Vietcong."

"I did," Cho nodded. "That is what resulted in his re-moval from office when the US leaned on our president to bring pressure on the communist element. He is well connected with the hill people who grow and harvest the poppies."

Similar to places like Latin America and the Middle East, the politics—and consequently, armed conflict—in Southeast Asia went hand in hand with the trafficking of illicit drugs. The US military, for instance, subsidized the poppy-growing, anti-Communist Montagnard tribes of the Central Highlands because they were a vital asset in their fierce opposition to the VC even though the Monts continued to cultivate and traffic in contraband as they had for more than a century.

McGavin said, "That urban assault vehicle is firepower to back up his sentries. It's like they're down there waiting for us."

"Now you understand why I pursued my investigation alone."

"Doesn't matter to me what their firepower is," growled McGavin. "We'll go in soft. We're here for Kelly and Dinh. We'll engage on our way out only if we have to."

Cho patted the Ingram strapped over his shoulder and held to his side. "With surprise and stealth on our side, we stand a good chance if we encounter trouble."

McGavin lowered his binoculars, unstrapped them from around his neck and set them inside the opened hatch door of the van parked behind them.

"Let's move out," he said.

They broke from the rocky crag and started a fast slip-slide descent through the trees crowding the grassy incline.

Lahn Cho thought, *We have the ability and the drive to succeed. Let us hope that's enough!* He concentrated on being in *this* moment, to be fully alive with no past and no future so as to maximize the potential of *now*.

As they soundlessly made their approach, Cho's confidence in himself and in the man beside him banished all apprehension. He feared failure more than he feared death though both shared equally in being a likely outcome of this dark op. It was an endeavor that many would justifiably call suicidal. But other than this mission tonight, what else was there for him?

The doctors and psychiatrists told him it was doubtful his wife, Anh, would ever return to the way she was before they lost their daughter. The part of his psychological makeup that was always looking for solutions had led him to read widely in the area of coping with the loss of a child. He'd learned that such a loss often caused irreparable damage to the relationship between the parents. It had certainly unfolded that way in his and Anh's case after the loss of their daughter. Their courtship—the bicycle rides through Saigon's beautiful parks and botanical gardens and along the scenic river shore—had deepened into the deepest, truest love there could ever be with marriage and the birth of little Chau.

So long ago. So *very* long ago.

Heavily sedated, Anh these days could barely function. With no interest in communicating with anyone, she spent most of her time in a catatonic trance, staring at the television whether it was turned on or not.

No one awaited Cho's return this or any night. So much for his foreseeable future. His past only fueled his hatred, not only for those responsible for Chau's death and Anh's fate but likewise for anyone like Ambrose who was in any way connected with this evil.

That was the only truth Cho lived for and he gave thanks to a higher power that he'd found an ally in Cord McGavin.

Would they locate the woman they sought behind these towering walls? Cho thought, *Woman?* The one they sought tonight was McGavin's *wife!* That was the reason he was willing to yield command of this operation to the American.

He and McGavin shared much in common besides rank and their military service. They'd both been cops before becoming soldiers. Seasoned law enforcement officers from anywhere in the world share an understanding of human nature, a bond that unites them with their own language, nuances and experience. Nighttime raids, undercover insertions and dangerous operations had always been part of Cho's work as a Saigon cop before the war, much as McGavin had worked his beat on American streets.

But more than anything, Cho knew it was the deepest bond between them. Each man was driven, risking everything and putting his life on the line for the woman he loved—Cho, driven to avenge the fate that had befallen his wife and daughter and McGavin, forging ahead to prevent such a fate befalling the woman who ruled his heart.

They gained the base of the wall, each man unfastening a climbing rope from his combat webbing.

The rain would work for them. It was always easier to penetrate a defensive setup like this when the elements were at their worst, when a sentry's inclination is to walk with head bent down against the rain and cold that has already chilled him to the bone.

Cho and McGavin stood side by side, several feet out from the wall. They twirled the climbing ropes over their heads for a fling at the top of the wall. Cho's metal-pronged rope end caught on the one-foot-wide brick. McGavin's rope fell back down. He caught it, tossed it again, and this time the prongs latched on. The two men started up the wall, pulling themselves while they "walked" up the side of the wall, hand over hand.

McGavin did not kid himself. This plan to rescue Kelly and neutralize Senator Dinh sounded like it might work. But it was a real long shot.

He'd counted three sentries at the gatehouse in the east wall and a walking three-man patrol, the only visible signs of a security presence from this distance. Security here had to be low profile, even with the numbers and fire-power. Dinh couldn't afford to advertise what he was up to. But there was the arrival of the urban assault vehicle. One always had to count on the worst happening. It was a good way to avoid being surprised.

He and Cho hoisted themselves atop the wall together, flattening out up there, each man hastily rewinding the climbing rope to reattach on his webbing.

The massive, three-level main house was well lit. Modern guest houses were lined near the wall but they were dark and the closest was two hundred meters east from the corner where McGavin and Cho paused.

What McGavin had not expected was to find the three-man sentry foot patrol passing by directly beneath them: three guys in security service uniforms. Except for their weaponry—assault rifles—and their shoul-

der-to-shoulder slogging through the rain with a semblance of military bearing, nothing stamped them as
moonlighting ARVN infantrymen.

The roiling, pregnant heavens chose that instant to sear
the black-cloud ceiling with a giant strobe light show that
lasted long enough to turn the gloom white, whiter than
sunlight. A barrage of thunder humped the atmosphere,
causing one of the sentries to idly glance up.

In that silver-rain lightning, he saw the two men atop
the wall.

Chapter 20

....

As time passed, Kelly talked herself into relaxing as best she could and not showing the urge to break free from her bonds. Her relaxing, apparently, had an effect on the man watching her. He too seemed to relax somewhat and, after what must have been an hour or two, he removed the blindfold and with one sharp yank he peeled off the electrical tape from her mouth.

Kelly emitted a reflexive yip of pain but showed no other reaction.

He was the man who had punched her in the Renault. A natural curl to the corner of his mouth gave him a permanent sneer. He returned to a chair identical to hers. Its front legs raised a few inches off the floor when he tilted back against the wall. He continued smoking and watching her without expression. This went on for some time.

Eventually, nature took its course.

Kelly said in Vietnamese, "Whoever you are . . . I need to pee." As was usual, a full bladder had diminished every emotion except irritability. "I don't know how long you expect me to sit like this and not pee."

His chuckle startled her.

"At last, you say something worth responding to." Chuong's conversational tone was both amused and dangerous. "You have to pee. This I like."

"Yes, well, now that I've amused you, would you please oblige me?"

Kelly wanted to scream and curse him out, the creep. But she'd broken the ice, drawing a response. She must keep her fear and outrage under wraps.

Chuong said, "I will do this."

It was a windowless ten-by-ten-foot room of high, blank cement walls. A single light bulb burned inside wire mesh attached to the ceiling. There was one door, across from where she sat. This was an unused storeroom.

But where?

Kelly gulped hard, hoping the gulp didn't sound as loud to him as it did inside her head.

She said, "Thank you. Really. Thank you! I really do need to pee so bad."

She was exaggerating. There was pressure in her bladder to pee making its presence known but she could have gone another hour or two, easily. Still, that slight pressure had given her this idea. Now, she wondered what she could do about it.

His sneer grew.

"So now you pee," he said. "You start now and do it. Do it!"

Kelly gulped again and she thought, *Uh oh.*

"Please, avert your eyes, won't you?"

He chuckled again and lit another cigarette. He spoke through exhaled smoke.

"Why should I?" Lewdness glinted in his eyes from behind the veil of smoke. The cigarette bobbed from the corner of his mouth. "Go on. Do it. I will watch you urinate. I like to watch."

Kelly's mind raced. What could she say? What could she do? She had found a way to get the blindfold removed. Could she find a way to . . . to what? Something flittered into her mind like a leaf carried in on a breeze. This creep was a kinky sicko and this was the only chance she had . . .

She lowered her chin in a subtle gesture of submission and looked at him through fluttering eyelashes.

"What makes you think I won't enjoy having you watch?"

The front legs of Chuong's chair snapped to the floor. He muttered something that sounded like a curse. He studied her as if for the first time.

Kelly batted her eyelashes at him some more.

"You heard me." She made her voice throaty, sultry. "I said I don't mind if you want to watch."

"Is that so?" Lewdness dripped from his words like oil. His eyes caressed her. The cigarette, dangling from the corner of his mouth, was half ash. He said, "Then do it. Let me see you pee, pretty American lady."

She thought, *All right, Kelly. You've gone this far, girl, don't stop now. The vamp approach is working. Go for it!*

She said in a small, pleading voice, "But you must untie me. Please. I don't want to soil my clothes. Please have mercy on me."

The pervert was enjoying himself immensely. He liked hearing her beg.

"And why should I?"

"Well . . ." She licked her dry lips with a darting tongue. "You would see more if you let me roll my pants down so I could do it. You'd like that, wouldn't you?"

Chuong's eyes narrowed. He did not reply but he was thinking about it.

Kelly's heart hammered against her ribcage as if someone was repeatedly kicking her from the inside and she felt herself breaking out in a cold, clammy sweat that she hoped didn't register as paleness. It was important that this perv thought she might really be into something like that. She nodded to indicate a coffee can next to his chair, into which he had been dropping his cigarette butts.

"Let me pee into that. Just untie me long enough for me to squat. Please. You," yet again she fluttered the eyelashes, "won't be disappointed."

Chuong made up his mind. A twist here and a pull there resulted in the clothesline falling away.

The cigarette smoke stung her eyes and clogged her nostrils but with the clothesline not binding her, she felt release like a bird taking wing.

Chuong stepped away and nudged the coffee can toward her with the toe of a boot. His laughter was a coarse, ugly thing.

"So do it. I wish I had a camera."

Kelly could not see even a shred of human decency in him. What choice did she have? She had never peed in front of anyone!

She gingerly drew the coffee can toward her like the repugnant object it was. She placed it between her ankles.

She loosened her slacks as if preparing to shift the material of her clothing and squatted.

Chuong watched her closely, absently drawing a fresh cigarette from the pack in his breast pocket. Holding the lighter in his other hand, he shifted his eyes from her only for the instant necessary to place the flame of the lighter against the tip of the cigarette.

In that split second, Kelly came up at him lightning fast. She pivoted with blinding speed, gripping the can in both hands and straightening out her arms. It was only a coffee can but the conditioned strength of her muscles and the pent-up rage drove the can to Chuong's forehead with all the power she could muster, knocking him off his feet, depositing him in a corner.

Kelly sprang for the door, grabbing at the door handle and twisting at it feverishly, yanking the door inward. She bolted out, hearing Chuong scramble to his feet after her.

She was free!

It was a windowless corridor with a pair of closed doors in the opposite wall. One end of the corridor door was a blank cement wall. At the other, a narrow, carpeted stairway led upstairs.

She was being held in the basement of . . . what? Where was she? Residence? Business establishment? Not that it mattered. She had to get away. She was determined. Focused. Without hesitation!

She sprinted toward the stairs. Chuong closed in fast from behind.

"Got you, you bitch!"

His voice was so close it sounded like it came from inside her head!

He launched himself into a running tackle, reaching

for her ankles. He brought Kelly down to the tiled floor. Ceiling and floor seemed to cartwheel around her in a wave of panic.

She twisted free, regaining her balance. Chuong regained his footing and advanced on her. Rage flushed his features. Kelly banished her panic, regaining her mental equilibrium. She assumed the martial stance Cord had taught her. As her opponent drew closer, she dropped to the side and lashed out with a foot, delivering a kick that caught Chuong in the abdomen. She'd intended the kick to land lower but it was enough to double him over. Chuong dropped to his knees, gasping for air.

Kelly whirled away to resume her escape. She didn't know enough to incapacitate the man permanently. Getting away was her only goal. But she froze in place at the unexpected, startling sight before her.

A man had arrived on her blind side while she was tangling with Chuong. He now stood at the foot of the narrow stairway. He was a lean man in his fifties, wearing reflector sunglasses. His facial features, hard and expressionless, could have been carved from stone.

He held a pistol in his right hand. His right arm was extended so that the muzzle of the gun was cold against her forehead, which was slick with perspiration. He spoke in Vietnamese.

"That will be quite enough of that, dear lady." Then he said over her shoulder to the man behind her, "You deserved that, Chuong, for letting her get the best of you."

"It won't happen again," said Chuong. He stepped forward and sneered at Kelly. "I hope you understand, bitch, that you may breathe and feel . . . but you're already dead. And this I promise: you will die screaming."

Chapter 21

....

Outside, in the night—

In that sustained moment of strobe lightning that ren-
dered the rainy scene into a surreal, metallic sort of daylight, two of the sentries passing beneath the wall did not
see McGavin and Cho, absorbed as they were in some
conversation of their own.

The middle man who had glanced up at the heavens
with a curse on his lips against the elements, the one who
saw the figures flattened atop the wall but not flat enough,
opened his mouth to yell a warning to his comrades.

McGavin and Cho triggered their Ingrams.

The MAC noise and flash suppressors kept the
weapons' reports down to a discreet chug that stitched
the three sentries into reverse gallops and their dead
back-stepping stopped at the base of the wall that was

already a mural of their sprayed guts. The only sounds were the violent flapping about of their bodies that bonked off the wall to fall facedown atop each other. Those sounds were muffled by the constant, sibilant hiss of rain kissing the ground.

No indications of a reaction came from the main house. The steady sound of the rain, the sheer breadth of the estate grounds, a line of guest houses, and the noise and flash suppressors combined to mute the sounds of the triple kill.

Something, though, was happening at the front of the house where the armored personnel carrier appeared, almost comically, out of place beneath the portico. There was nothing funny, though, about the M-50 mounted behind the cab.

A squad of ARVN troopers had disembarked from the confines of the armored vehicle. They stood under the cover of the portico, away from the rain, smoking cigarettes.

A Viet officer in his mid-thirties strutted out of the main front entrance of Dinh's home, snapping orders at the soldiers who doused their smokes. They deployed in pairs in various directions, along with members of the security force that had joined them from inside the house. They dispersed to distant positions around the wall to prepare their ambush for whenever McGavin showed up.

McGavin said, "Let's get a move on while we can."

"My sentiments precisely," said Cho.

They sprang off the top of the wall together in loose drops that landed them safely in somersaulting rolls, each man coming up onto his feet on the landscaped terrace inside the wall.

McGavin indicated the sprawled bodies.

"Let's stash this bunch first."

They hurried over to the tangle of unmoving arms and legs that were the remains of the sentries. An inky clutch of shrubbery grew to nearly six-feet high between where the killings took place and the nearest of those guest houses. Moving together with an absolute economy of movement, they grabbed the arms and legs, tugging the corpses and their dropped weapons into the deepest shadows around the shrubs.

Cho observed with understated coolness, "We have trouble."

McGavin turned from surveying the results of having stuffed the dead men from sight. He saw what Cho saw.

A guy in pilot gear had waltzed out the back door of the main house, strutting over to board the helicopter.

Cho said, "Colonel Ambrose was double-crossed," said Cho, "and now that the deal has gone down . . . is that the expression?"

"That's it," said McGavin.

"Now that Dinh has everything he wants, there is no reason not to vacate these premises. We must stop him. We will never get another chance like this."

"And he's liable to take Kelly with him," McGavin growled more to himself than to Cho. "Let's go!"

The noise of the bubble-front starting up shook the night, louder than the rain.

McGavin and Cho trotted off together from the clump of shrubs that blended with the tastefully landscaped acreage that separated their corner of the wall from the main house.

The helicopter pilot did not spot them, being far too

occupied with his controls in preparing for imminent takeoff. The small chopper waited there, its rotor blades *whishhhing* in the rain.

McGavin and Cho gained a darkened corner of the main house, where they paused out of the pelting rain around the corner from the helicopter and blocked from the sight of anyone else by the line of guest houses.

The ground floor row of windows along this side of Dinh's mansion was dark except for a door, a screen door, from which came a rectangle of indirect light that refracted falling raindrops. The screen door was off a patio bordered by well-tended flower beds. Voices could be heard in terse conversation from inside, through the screen door. The words were not audible enough to be understood.

McGavin motioned Cho ahead with him. They soundlessly made their way through the senator's flower beds, hugging the wall of the house. Each man held his Ingram close in but aimed out, ready to unleash more silent death.

McGavin paused with his back pasted to the rain-slimed brick, several feet from the screen door. Satisfied that he and Cho remained undetected, he continued to ease along the wall a couple of careful inches had a time.

Cho eyed their backtrack and the impenetrable gloom around them. Dinh's security force was apparently now in position along the wall, their attention and weaponry directed outward. The hidden bodies of the sentries had not been discovered. The night and the rain were a big help.

McGavin concentrated on getting closer to the screen door. He sensed vibrations in the atmosphere. There was no other word for it. Less than five minutes had passed since they'd topped the wall and extinguished the lives of those three sentries. They'd penetrated to the very heart of Dinh's estate which was now nothing less than a fortified trap ready to be sprung. That fact, more than any other, confirmed in McGavin's mind that they had Kelly and this was where they knew he would show up looking for her. He and Cho had made it this far.

But their luck could not last . . .

Chapter 22

....

With only his basic knowledge of the Viet language to draw on, McGavin concentrated on eavesdropping, his ear as close as he dared to the screen door. Cho made a wide circle around the light from inside to take up position on the opposite side of the door. An overhang partially shielded them from the rain.

Inside, a male voice was speaking.

"And so, Chuong, all is in order?"

It was a voice of command with the cool, clipped cadence of authority.

Chuong replied, "Yes, sir. Security is in place along the wall, waiting for this man, McGavin. If he has not appeared by sunrise, we will assume he has chosen another time and place to engage us. But whether he strikes here now or later, senator, rest assured that my men are ready for him."

McGavin knew the next voice quite well. It belonged to Kelly.

"You're ready for Cord McGavin?" she said with a sneer of contempt. "Guess what, chumps? When my husband comes calling, he'll be *more* than ready and you'll *never* be ready for the hammer he's going to drop on your sorry asses."

McGavin couldn't resist an inward grin. *Yup, he'd found his Kelly.*

He knelt beside the screen door, lowering his head to the cold, wet pavement. Then he inched an eye around the corner of the doorframe, far below anyone's normal line of vision, to survey the interior from ground level.

Three people stood in the private library. McGavin's impression was that they'd just walked in.

The lean guy in the reflector shades had to be Senator Dinh. *The son of a bitch had what looked like a tight grip on Kelly's wrist!* Chuong, holding a submachine gun, stood between an impressive mahogany desk and a wall of books, allowing him to cover Kelly with the machine gun without getting close enough for her to strike out, something she looked wholly capable and angry enough to do.

Dinh laughed.

"Listen to you. What your American males would call the little woman voicing hope that is only a dream." Dinh snickered. "If your husband wishes to stay alive, he will not set foot on this property. And if he does, the odds will be twenty to one against him. No man stands a chance against that."

Kelly said, "We'll see."

Dinh released her with a shove that deposited Kelly

in a wing chair. She massaged her bruised wrist and eyed Dinh venomously.

Dinh resumed addressing Chuong.

"After McGavin is dealt with, there will, naturally, be a response from the local authorities. They are in my pocket and the payoff is arranged. When they arrive, any formality will be glossed over in the interest of maintaining appearances. See that they get no closer than the front gate. After they're gone, take care of the bodies as was done with Ambrose."

Chuong smacked his lips noisily. His eyes were undressing Kelly inch by inch.

"Yes," he said, "but I will *use* her body before I kill her. I will take her and—"

"Enough," snapped Dinh. "Whatever happens, your convoy will leave here at sunup."

"Yes, sir."

"Authorization has been arranged. You have your orders of transit?"

Chuong drew his eyes away from Kelly but only with effort.

"The merchandise will be transported in broad daylight to the staging area in the country," he assured Dinh.

"A busy time of day," Dinh nodded. "The start of a workday in a city at war, the streets and roads clogged. You'll be just another convoy traveling with government authorization and protection."

"The armored personnel carrier will provide security," said Chuong. "I have personally double-checked every detail."

McGavin withdrew from the screen door. He'd heard enough. *It's now or never,* he thought. *The three of them are well-separated. Dinh has to be armed certainly but his hands are empty at the moment. Kelly is well out of any line of fire that would take out the two men.* The gunman, Chuong, was the primary target. He and that machine gun of his had to be taken down as the first order of business. Dinh, Chuong and Kelly were absorbed in the interplay of their drama.

Yeah.

Now or never.

He sent Cho the briefest nod which the ARVN man returned as if reading McGavin's mind. Cho had his buddy's back.

Then McGavin rose and left his concealment. Turning, he planted himself squarely in the rectangle of light from the screen door that fell upon the ground at his feet. A single powerful kick punched the screen door inward off its hinges. He stepped inside, bringing up the MAC-10 in target acquisition on Chuong, knowing that Cho would be fanning out behind him for a line of fire.

McGavin squeezed the trigger.

Nothing.

Jammed!

It was a rare but ever-present possibility and the worst thing that could happen in combat unless you're the soldier in Chuong's position who finds himself cheating the fickle finger of fate. Chuong registered that stunned expression of one certain he was about to die, then finding himself alive. His befuddlement lasted for only a heartbeat, promptly replaced by snarling, savage rage directed at the one who'd come so close to killing him. Chuong's machine gun swung on McGavin.

But that heartbeat of delay provided time enough for

McGavin to throw away the useless piece of crap Ingram and pitch himself forward onto the floor, pawing for his sidearm.

Chuong fired, the blast of his machine gun filling the library with cataclysmic thunder. Bullets riddled the wall behind where McGavin had stood seconds earlier. Without taking his finger from the trigger, Chuong lowered his aim to catch up with McGavin's lightning-fast evasion.

Cho suddenly materialized, standing in the doorway. He caressed a three-round burst from his Ingram that was like an invisible high-velocity cannonball blowing out the whole middle of Chuong's chest, belching red mud out of the exit wounds in his back, his innards preceding him as the force of the burst flung him to the floor, totally dead.

Gunfire barked from outside, ricochets whistling off the exterior of the house. Cho whirled, hitting a crouch away from the light from the door to return fire. In the library, McGavin was back on his feet, tracking the .45 up in a two-handed stance, his thumb flicking off the safety. He held his fire, the .45's muzzle aimed directly at Dinh's forehead.

Senator Dinh and Kelly now stood less than ten feet before him, Dinh having again yanked Kelly to her feet. He stood behind her, an arm across her throat forcefully holding her in place as a human shield. Dinh had drawn a concealed weapon. The pistol's snout was pressed to Kelly's temple.

She said, "Hello, Cord," in a calm voice. "I was sort of expecting you to show up."

Cord's chuckle was hard-edged.

"So I gather."

Even under these circumstances, in her scuffed, disarrayed clothing she looked beautiful to McGavin. Kelly's red hair was tousled, partially covering her face. She stood there with her knees slightly bent, barely noticeable. Noticeable to McGavin, though. To McGavin, she looked like a cat ready to spring.

Dinh spoke to McGavin over Kelly's shoulder.

"Ah. Major. At last, you put in an appearance. I was concerned that the weather might dissuade you."

McGavin did not lower the .45.

"You wanted me, senator, and you damn well got me. Now, stop hiding behind that woman. This is between you and me. The two of us. Let her go. Let's get down with it, just you and me."

"You may hold a gun on me, Major," Dinh said in a reasonable voice, "but I hold this woman with a gun to her head. Drop your weapon, McGavin. I will not hesitate to kill her."

Chapter 23

....

"Throw down my gun so you can kill me?" McGavin shook his head. "I don't think so." To Kelly, he said with a small smile, "How's the *chi*, babe?"

It was more than a year since they'd last worked out together, practicing her moves. But her response now was immediate.

Kelly said, "My *chi* is on and ready.

A frown creased Dinh's features. The exchange between Cord and Kelly was like a private joke or a secret, so natural and seemingly spontaneous that it gave Dinh no time to react. He started to snarl his displeasure.

McGavin did not give him the chance. He holstered the .45. He had no doubt Dinh would pull the trigger if he felt it was necessary. McGavin hadn't gone through all the crap he had to get here just so he could witness Kelly getting her brains blown out. No, there was another way to take Dinh down without more bullets being fired in here.

He said to Kelly, "Do something, hon. Anything. Get this ball rolling."

He was projecting a call he didn't feel. Gunfire continued from outside where Cho was trading fire with Dinh's men who were coming to the senator's aid. McGavin had to deal with Dinh without delay in the library. Cho would be needing his help outside.

Kelly did not disappoint.

She executed a sharp jab of her elbow, lifting her arm as much as she could in Dinh's hold so that the elbow sharply struck the side of his head, jarring the gun barrel away from her head as Dinh's head snapped back. He bellowed in rage, in pain, releasing his hold on her. Kelly lunged aside.

Dinh forgot about Kelly, tracking his pistol in Mc-Gavin's direction, snap-firing.

McGavin was already charging, weaving and dodging. Dinh's bullet ricocheted off the opposite wall. McGavin launched himself into a flying dropkick, slamming the heel of one foot into Dinh's chest. The other foot smashed into the senator's face in a terrific piston kick that sent both men heavily into the wall, knocking the pistol from Dinh's hand.

Dinh assumed a martial stance, throwing a reverse punch that would have taken the uninitiated by surprise because it was delivered with the hand on the same side as the rear foot. McGavin evaded the punch with a right block. Dinh shifted his weight and feinted, a deceptively clumsy lunge that exposed his chest and belly invitingly. McGavin refused the bait. Dinh laughed and turned and

McGavin turned with him.

"Are you ready to die, American?" Dinh taunted. The silver lenses of his aviator sunglasses reflected the library's lights. "I will kill you, then I will take this bitch of yours and when I have finished, I will leave what's left to my men for their amusement."

McGavin said, "You talk too much."

Dinh grunted, stepping in fast. McGavin dropped to the side, delivering a reverse elbow strike that caught Dinh in the mouth. Gasping and with blood dribbling from his mouth, the senator stumbled again. Snarling with pain and anger, he pivoted with surprising speed to lash out with another kick as McGavin closed in. The force of the kick to his chest drove McGavin backward into the wall of books. With a shout of triumph, Dinh rushed him.

McGavin drove a hard right cross to the senator's face, knocking him to the floor. He was on him in a flash, grabbing Dinh's arms above the elbows. He rammed a knee into Dinh's abdomen. Dinh gasped breathlessly from the blow but he managed to snap his head forward so he could butt his forehead at McGavin's face. The blow missed its mark. Frontal bone struck frontal bone. Both men were dazed but McGavin was more stunned as the recipient of the head butt.

Dinh broke free of McGavin's grip. He seized McGavin's throat with both hands and McGavin felt the guy's thumbs digging into his windpipe. Dinh's fingers pressed into the carcinoid arteries in his neck. McGavin clasped his hands together and thrust them between Dinh's arms, his elbows striking the senator's wrists. The fingers popped away from his throat, allowing McGavin to chop his hands in a short, downward stroke that smashed Dinh across the bridge of his nose.

Dinh almost lost his reflector shades, staggering back from the blow. McGavin slugged him with a hard left hook that hardly slowed him down. Dinh managed to lash out a boot kick that caught McGavin in his left hip. McGavin gasped, nearly losing his balance.

The sudden rattle of close-up auto-fire in the library caused him to duck instinctively, whipping his attention around just in time to see Kelly spray bullets from Chuong's Ingram at a Viet gunman who'd appeared in the patio doorway. The man was flung back by the impacting bullets. Kelly's whole body continued shuddering from the weapon's recoil even after she stopped firing.

McGavin thought, *Cho's defending that approach. How did this guy get this close? Shit!*

McGavin back-fisted Dinh's face, followed up by a side-kick to the senator's chest that put Dinh down onto the floor, the wind knocked out of him. Dinh appeared woozy, driven to continue but unsteady from the battering McGavin was dishing out. Dinh glared murderously at McGavin and struggled to regain his footing.

Movement stirred in the patio doorway to McGavin's left. Unleathering the .45, he pumped a pair of hot sizzlers into the torso of another Viet gunman who died on his feet, toppling across the first body.

Kelly offered the Ingram to McGavin.

"Here, you want this?"

Taking the machine gun, he handed her the .45, then spent precious seconds liberating a couple of fresh ammo magazines from Chuong's corpse. The Ingram's barrel was hot and smoking. He ejected the spent clip, feeding in the fresh magazine with a slap of his palm.

"Stay close," he said to Kelly. "This is a tough neighborhood."

"Don't worry about that," said Kelly. "Worry about *him!*"

Dinh had regained his footing, finally minus his reflector shades. He shook his head, trying to clear it. Then his dazed focus settled on them. He started toward them but he was sluggish. His hands were rising unsteadily for physical combat. Winded but determined, he was still plenty dangerous.

McGavin shifted the Ingram to his left hand as he and Kelly hustled toward the patio doorway. He tugged one of the hand grenades from the webbing beneath his jacket. Lifting the grenade in his right fist, he unplugged the detonator with his teeth. From close behind him he heard the nasty bark of the .45. He could only hope Kelly was taking out another of Dinh's goons. McGavin was busy gauging aim and distance.

He pitched the grenade, an overhand speedball with the accuracy of a baseball pitcher on the mound. It was the last he saw of Dinh—the grenade popping the senator right in the forehead, packing enough punch to knock Dinh off his feet yet again while McGavin took a running leap over the bodies in the doorway.

Kelly was nowhere in sight.

It was all happening *very* fast.

Then the earth shook with a mighty *BLAMMM!* that rocked the house and the night. The detonation punched glass out of windows. Sizable splinters of the big oak desk razored the air every which way, and millions of tattered pages of books fluttered and settled like snow. McGavin thought he heard one terrified scream that could have been Dinh but he couldn't be sure and didn't give a damn.

The rain had let up but the world remained an impenetrable place of gloom. Shouting in the near distance from the direction of the walls and from the front gate could be heard through the steady *drip-drip-drip* of water droplets from surrounding tree limbs and leaves. Men were urgently shouting questions of concern out there in the blackness.

There was no sign of Cho or Kelly.

McGavin eyed his backtrack. The walls and ceiling of the library were an ugly mess of blood, tattered bits of clothing and body parts that belonged to what had been the traitor Dinh Quang.

A pair of Dinh's security men arrived in a hurry in the library's opposite doorway. They saw McGavin and pulled up their rifles fast but not fast enough. McGavin triggered a medium-length burst from the Ingram, sending a hail of flesh-eaters buzzing across the library's ruins. And the two fell dead.

Then came Kelly's faint summons from the far side of the patio.

"Cord . . . over here . . ."

He cautiously advanced toward the weak voice, weak only because Kelly didn't want to draw anyone else's attention to where McGavin found her in the deepest shadows.

Cho lay stretched out upon the cold, damp ground. Kelly knelt, cradling his head. It took only one look in the faint light from the shattered screen door to see that Cho was a goner. As McGavin had feared, his Viet counterpart had been hit while defending that doorway. Cho's chest was a bloody, pulped mess. He shivered like a man with terrible chills. Blood bubbled from his nose and mouth.

When Cho realized it was McGavin, he lifted his head as best he could.

"The senator?" he asked, the words nearly inaudible through the gurgling blood.

"Dead as they come," said McGavin.

Cho somehow summoned the strength to rest a hand on McGavin's shoulder. His next words came slightly stronger.

He said, "Please . . . tell my wife I love her."

And he died.

McGavin grimaced with a sharp spasm of the psyche. Cho was here tonight, meeting his end because McGavin had invited him on this life-or-death mission. Death for Cho. McGavin's next thought was the realization that, given Cho's own agenda to bring Dinh down after what happened to his daughter, Cho would have no doubt insisted on being included if McGavin hadn't made him the offer. McGavin's instincts rebelled at the very idea of leaving Cho's body behind on enemy ground. But the whole reason for this hit, and Cho's sacrifice, was to take down Dinh's heroin smuggling operation and extract Kelly. Mc-Gavin had made a promise to a dying man whose remains would soon enough receive the proper attention when this place became overrun by US and ARVN authorities and that would happen within minutes.

The only objective now was to extract Kelly and himself.

Chapter 24

....

The racket of motorized conveyances—not real vehicles, more like golf carts—could be heard departing from the main gate. These would, no doubt, contain the security staff, who would be deploying them in a defensive reflex, rushing the main house in force with the rogue ARVN troopers, heading toward the main entrance beneath the portico on the other side of the house.

McGavin turned to fire a parting burst into the library to give anyone back there second thoughts. Then he and Kelly hurried to a rear corner of the house.

He was troubled at not hearing engine noise from the armored personnel carrier out there in the night. Likely it was keeping a low profile, having been requisitioned to provide daytime transportation camouflage for Dinh's truckload of contraband. *Where was the damn thing now?*

A golf cart came two-wheeling on rain-slick grass around the nearest corner, its single headlight stabbing ahead like a luminous knife.

McGavin took out the driver without hesitation, zipping a tight pattern of slugs that chucked the guy out of the cart. The cart sailed on, driverless for a few seconds before swerving into the side of the house.

Kelly hurried over to switch off the cart's headlight. McGavin chanced a glance around the corner.

The helicopter sat about fifteen yards away. A military half-ton truck, its bed sealed with a tarp, sat on a gravel patch near the helipad. This would be the transport vehicle for the contraband. Currently, it sat by itself, lights and engine off, unmanned.

Aboard the small chopper, the pilot, sitting at the controls, was staring expectantly toward a side door of the house, obviously unaware of Senator Dinh's fate. The chopper's engine rumbled loud enough to drown any noise of the batter, so the pilot had not heard it. It had been noisy enough to stir up the rest of the force on the grounds, sure, but not noisy enough to penetrate to the pilot through the sound of the helicopter's engine. Only ninety seconds had elapsed since the action in the library.

McGavin discerned two figures on foot emerge around a far corner, silhouetted against refracted light from the front of the house, drawn by the crash of the cart into the back side of the structure.

McGavin stepped away from the corner, motioning Kelly to stay where she was. Kelly obeyed. She watched McGavin assume a shooter's crouch, one arm extended to partially shield her from possible incoming return fire. Another couple of men had joined the first group. Mc-

Gavin's auto-burst from the Ingram kicked three of that cluster through the pearly gates, their chests punctured with bullet holes. The survivors scrambled for cover. McGavin palmed a fresh magazine into the smoking Ingram. He grasped Kelly's right wrist.

They dashed across open ground toward the helicopter.

As they ran past the half-ton, McGavin shouted, "Tires."

Kelly didn't need to be told twice. Without slacking pace, she fired two bullets apiece into the truck's front and rear tires on its passenger side. The half-ton settled on its left side, effectively disabled and ready for discovery by the proper authorities.

The pilot, a middle-aged Viet civilian, was still eyeing the house having become aware that something was wrong. He jerked his face around when he realized he'd been taken by a half-seen apparition that dragged him from the bubble front.

McGavin flung him to the wet ground. In case the guy was nothing more than a civilian contractor, a victim of circumstance, he intended to leave the man and then hope like hell he remembered his unschooled flight experience from AIT several lifetimes ago.

But the idiot pilot revealed his allegiance. He reached for and produced a pistol, murder in his eyes. That was as far as he got. McGavin lunged in, delivering a killing judo chop that caved in the back of the pilot's skull behind the left ear, collapsing him to the ground with two trickles of crimson snaking from his nostrils. Dead eyes rolled back into his head.

McGavin heaved himself aboard the small helicopter. He hurriedly studied its dash with a furrowed brow. The little copter's controls seemed fairly basic compared to the military jobs he'd flown and worked on. Tentatively, he reached for a switch and gave it a flick. He sighed his relief when the rotor blades increased.

When Kelly climbed into the passenger seat, she retained a firm grip on McGavin's .45.

"Don't tell me you can fly this thing!"

"Let's find out," said McGavin.

He revved the chopper's turbines. The metal bird started vibrating, the rotors chopping around at increasing RPMs, whipping the mist out from the copter's backwash like a small hurricane. Then, its treads were lifting off the slippery turf.

McGavin told himself, *Hell, it's like riding a bicycle or driving a car once you know how!*

Riflemen ran around from in front of the house but were already receding from beneath the rising chopper. Some of their bullets started spanking the helicopter. McGavin used his right hand to control the copter while bringing the Ingram around to bear on the soldiers below. They had automatic weapons and, even in the dark, for the next handful of critical seconds, he and Kelly were literally sitting ducks. He squeezed the Ingram's trigger.

And nothing happened.

The Ingram jammed in his fist!

"Twice in one day?" he snarled. "This I do not believe!"

McGavin pitched the weapon out of the chopper. Working the controls, he banked the chopper toward the northwest wall of the estate.

Below, the armored personnel carrier finally made its presence known with an angry automotive grumble, spewing a cloud of diesel exhaust heavy enough to bite through the damp, overripe atmosphere. But those pin-point flashes of gunfire from below did not stop.

The chopper gained the north wall, the scene on the ground yielding into the rainy dark backdrop. McGavin was flying low at no more than fifteen feet. That would be just enough to safely clear the wall.

The low, throaty hammering of the personnel carrier's M-50 joined the rifle fire receding in their wake.

Kelly braced herself with her free arm extended, her palm pressed against the Plexiglas of the bubble front, keeping herself cool and collected but anyone could see the stress.

She said, "Are we going to make it, hon?"

McGavin's eyes were narrow, cold as steel, and his knuckles were white at the copter's controls.

"Cross your fingers, babe. One lucky round and—"

They both felt the sudden lurch of the aircraft when the *un*lucky round hit. The copter began tilting crazily.

"Got us!" growled McGavin.

The engine noises stopped altogether; only the airy *whirrrr* of the rotors could be heard as they plummeted down.

Chapter 25

....

Kelly was certain she was a heartbeat away from her own death.

Then the copter impacted but the jolt had a *spring!* to it, not the hard crash of slamming into earth she'd expected.

McGavin had landed the chopper in the fronds of a tree upon the incline outside of the wall, not far from where he and Cho had left their van less than fifteen minutes earlier. He'd trusted his sense of direction when steering the helpless aircraft along its natural downward path after passing over the wall.

And now, he trusted his nose when it pinched at the hard bite of fuel fumes. He'd been maintaining treetop altitude but the abrupt dissent when that round took out the rotor mechanism had dropped them just enough to rupture a fuel line.

"Jump for it!" he snarled, already unlatching his side of the bubble front.

Kelly bailed from the opposite side of the bubble front. McGavin left the helicopter, dropping from treetop level. They hit the ground together.

The rattling of gunfire had ceased from inside the walls of the estate. With the rain having stopped, the world was a quieter place, where men's voices calling to each other could be heard distinctly.

McGavin and Kelly hurried to get away from the tree that held the chopper. Then, muffled by rows of trees, the treed helicopter disintegrated into a sunburst of white-hot, orange-silver sparks and a loud *ka-boooom!*

They continued on to where the van waited. McGavin and Kelly boarded the van, McGavin pausing only a moment to shed the military webbing of grenades, ammo, and other gear worn beneath his jacket. The penetration gear got stashed on the floor behind the driver's seat. Kelly handed him back his .45. He reloaded the pistol with a fresh magazine before leathering the piece in its underarm holster, then he slipped on the light jacket again.

McGavin popped the clutch and sent the vehicle bounding forward, keeping only the amber parking lights on to follow the contours of the winding trail through the night.

From this higher ground, they could hear and partially see the unbridled confusion unfurling down below on the estate grounds. The security force and the ARVN soldiers flitted around here and there, reminding McGavin of a big chicken that had lost its head. A damn fine metaphor considering that Senator Dinh—the head man who paid them (that being the only reason they were involved)—was now nothing more than fresh bloodstains and scattered body parts in his home library. And dead men don't pay.

McGavin wheeled the van onto the two-lane blacktop, the most direct route back into the urban sprawl of Saigon. They crested a hill and were then driving past Dinh's home.

The damage there had been done. It would be a crazy scene within those walls, the bunch inside far too preoccupied with the hellstorm that had just gone down to notice or react to a van driving by.

McGavin waited until that property was in their rearview before depressing the van's accelerator to the floorboard. Kelly had certainly demonstrated her ability to defend herself but her safety and nothing else remained his only concern.

They had not gone more than half a kilometer when the first emergency vehicles, their rooftop lights flashing, sirens wailing, whistled past them, heading in the opposite direction toward the battleground that had erupted out of nowhere, or so it had seemed, in the exclusivity of this quiet countryside. More sirens could be heard filling the night like animal howls, rushing this way from every direction.

McGavin brought his speed down to normal. Just another unmarked, nondescript van tooling along at a modest speed, minding its own business. The bad guys would have no time to fade away before the authorities arrived. It didn't matter what Dinh's prior bribes had supposedly bought him. Machine-gun fire and a crashing helicopter were something else and could not be ignored. The Viet cops would find dirty ARVN troops, Vietcong terrorists, who knew how many bodies, and an incapacitated truck loaded with heroin—all on the grounds of an ex-senator. That should be more than enough to keep everyone busy.

They traveled in silence for a considerable time and distance, Kelly sitting erect, staring straight ahead. She looked composed from the outside but McGavin knew better.

This was not his first rodeo, not here in Saigon nor that battle in the highlands and more than once as a city cop back in the World. He knew what it meant to take another's life. It always took something out of you, not only the tension and explosion of violence but also the psychic aftermath of having slaughtered other human beings no matter how just the cause, how necessary the act. McGavin would always remember his first time he canceled out a human life, a nowhere street punk coming at him with a shiv during what should have been a routine takedown. The young McGavin had been emotionally and spiritually winded for close to a week back then. All these years later he could still recall details of the instant it happened.

That's the sort of thing Kelly was sorting through now and so he let her. The shrinks would call it shock and that was sure true enough. He knew of his wife's close encounters with violence during her photojournalist work stateside both before and after they'd met and married. It was no understatement to say the woman could handle herself. But yeah, she was processing, bringing the primal intensity of kill-or-be-killed survival back to this semblance of normalcy.

A man and woman driving along in a van. Sure. *With the scent of battle and blood still clinging to them . . .*

After time passed, Kelly exhaled an extended breath. "Damn. I'm glad *that's* over."

McGavin assessed, *Voice steady. Reaction and thoughts*

lucid. She'll make it. She'd be fine.

He said, "You're safe, hon. But it won't be over until I put in my report and after I pay a call on Cho's wife."

"I love you, Cord."

"That's something I've learned to live with," he said. "And have I told you lately that you're certainly hell on wheels in a tight fight? Babe, I'm glad we're on the same side."

"Me too."

"This war will end one of these days," he said, "one way or another. But the stink of traitors like Ambrose and Dinh, that'll never be over."

"Did you say Colonel Ambrose?"

McGavin nodded. "Several bottom feeders got what they deserved back there. The colonel was one of them."

She took another minute or two to process that. McGavin didn't blame her. It had been one hell of a night.

Then she asked, "Where are we going?"

"After what you've been through," McGavin said, "you're getting proper medical attention. First stop is the ER at the base hospital."

"Sounds good."

"Then it's to CID HQ where I can start everyone's day off with a whole lot of news."

"What are you going to tell them?"

"What went down. And about Cho. Our people need to get in on the action at Dinh's ASAP."

"What about *us*, Cord? What about *me*?"

"Guess I need to put some thought into that one," he admitted.

They were nearing the lights of the sprawling American base. The main gate was in sight.

"I hope you're not going to come clean about us," said Kelly, "about all the rules I broke to get over here."

McGavin grimaced.

"Back home, people are dodging the draft. But my woman has to move heaven and earth to put herself smack dab in the middle of all this."

"And for the same reason."

"How's that?"

"We're both answering the call, you and me," she said. "Each in our own way. What's happening in Southeast Asia today matters to us because it matters to the path civilization is on. We want to *do* something, dammit. And after tonight, bub, I'd say I've earned the right to stay on the job in-country and continue."

"Bub?"

"That's what I want, Cord. I want to go on being Kelly Carpenter. It's up to you. They'd send me packing in a heartbeat if you tell them the truth about us."

"Yes, they would do that."

"Am I Kelly Carpenter or am I Kelly McGavin?"

"That's the problem," grunted McGavin. "You're both."

She wasn't pleading, wasn't begging. Not Kelly. Not ever. She spoke calmly, concisely stating the facts.

She'd roll with his decision, whichever way it came down. He knew Kelly well enough to know that. And yeah, it was *his* call and no one else's. The sight of his wife wielding a submachine gun, mowing down one of Dinh's gunmen in the library, was an image that would remain tattooed on McGavin's brain for the rest of his life. And it told him everything he needed to know about the woman he'd married.

McGavin gradually reduced their speed several hundred yards short of the main gate, gliding to a routine stop.

Routine that is, except for the fact that the van bore no official or commercial markings. And there was the early hour and it had been drummed into every sentry from the beginning of time that the hours preceding dawn are when an attack is most likely. A general heightening of security was still in effect following the Tet offensive but an attack could just as easily come from the *mama-san* delivering a basket of laundry that hid a bomb; the attacker could be that friendly shoeshine boy offering to buff your boots only to get close enough to use a handgun at short range.

And so, the main gate was manned by no-nonsense MPs and marines who observed the van's occupants with fingers curled around the trigger of their M16s.

McGavin identified himself, citing the CID detachment HQ as his destination.

The MP at his window kept his hand on the butt of a holstered sidearm. He shone his flashlight beam on the woman who sat in the bucket seat next to McGavin, staring straight ahead, mute.

"Who's this?"

McGavin was a soldier, yes. Duty, obeying orders, that was his life now as it had been when he'd been a cop in civilian life. It was the life he'd chosen. But he was also a *man*, by God, defined by *how* he lived. And how he loved. Kelly was right. She'd earned the right to be here and she'd damn right saved his life with that submachine gun. McGavin owed her.

He told the MP, "She's a journalist. Her name is Kelly Carpenter."

Fragged

....

(short story)

Quang Ngai Province, north of Saigon

The Huey gunship banked in over Firebase Tiger, a clearing carved from the jungle hilltop. The woman, who was calling herself Kelly Carpenter, began snapping pictures from the open side door of the helicopter, from behind the shoulder of the door gunner and his big, mounted M60 machine gun.

The landing zone was a barren five acres. After the stark green carpet of jungle they'd flown over from Saigon, this base was drab and squalid. There were no trees, no color except for the coating of red dust that blanketed everything: bunkers, vehicles and personnel. Machine-gun emplacements were at intervals along the perimeter. Artillery and mortars were inside the compound. The sun, like an angry red ball seen through the gauze of a humid haze, was arcing low in the west, painting the horizon a brilliant vermillion. This all vanished behind a veil of red dust, a sandstorm kicked up by the chopper's backwash as the pilot touched the Huey down gently and initiated the system's shutdown.

Kelly's fellow passenger stood beside her.

He said, "Getting enough pretty pictures for the war protestors back home?"

McGavin did not wait for a response. He left the gunship to stride toward a welcoming committee of three waiting soldiers. He wore fatigues and a shoulder holstered Colt .45 automatic.

Kelly, who also wore fatigues, chose not to respond to his sarcasm. She caught up as McGavin reached the trio of waiting soldiers.

The ranking man stepped forward. He had the build and the leathery features of a farmer, thirtyish, with a sunburned crewcut and flinty eyes. He did not salute. Enemy snipers loved to disrupt the chain of command and seeing who was saluted made selecting targets easy for them. Therefore, saluting was avoided in the field.

"Major, I'm Captain Larson, Executive Officer in Charge. Welcome to Firebase Tiger, though I imagine you'd rather be someplace else."

The man next to Larson was a strapping man with a coffee latte complexion and E-6 stripes on his sleeve.

"That goes for every mother's son in this hellhole, sir."

Larson said, "Easy, Top. Major, this is Sergeant Hines. He's my top shirt."

"I know," said McGavin. "I studied your personnel files on the flight in."

Hines kept shifting his attention between them and scanning the darkening jungle beyond the perimeter.

The third man was a First Lieutenant named Grey and everything about him matched his name. Blond-haired, in his late twenties, the junior officer was pale, almost albino-like except for a purple, swollen area around a bandage at his right temple.

Grey said, "Sergeant Hines speaks the truth. I wish I'd never heard of Firebase Tiger."

McGavin said, "You have a colonel who was fragged."

Larson nodded. "Lieutenant Colonel Emmett, 13th Infantry Battalion. Someone tossed a hand grenade into his hooch just before dawn today and splashed the walls with his guts."

"Hooch" was GI slang for makeshift living quarters. "Fragging" was another recently coined term. Bad command decisions by an officer too often got good soldiers killed. Sometimes an officer's own men, considering it more an act of survival than murder, would toss a grenade into the officer's hooch, blowing that officer into itty bitty officer fragments—"frag" him, in other words—before the officer got anyone else killed.

"Where's the body now?

Larson said, "What was left of it was tagged and bagged and sent back to Saigon on the daily chopper run."

Hines eyed McGavin. "One thing you ought to know up front, sir. Don't expect anyone on this base to feel bad about what happened."

Grey cleared his throat and nodded at Kelly. "Uh, if you don't mind, Major, who is she?"

"Her? Name's Carpenter. Photojournalist from the States. Pretend she's not here. Okay, Captain, show me where the fragging took place."

Larson led them toward a squalid, dust-covered pile of sandbags that was somewhat bigger than the other hooches.

"The colonel's hooch was next to the main bunker."

Kelly commenced taking pictures.

Activity swirled around them: a world of coarse language, exhaust fumes and the clicking and clanking of engines, equipment and weaponry. Nearly every soldier in sight was toting an M16 and a wary attitude. The shadows of encroaching night deepened by the minute.

The colonel's hooch was a low, ten-by-twelve, makeshift structure of timber and plywood beneath a shell of sandbags. Its entrance was charred, misshapen from the force of the murderous blast. McGavin stooped and entered while the others grouped outside.

The walls were splashed with gore and flies buzzed, thick and loud. The sickly-sweet smell of death was almost overpowering in the enclosed space.

"Did anyone see anything?"

Larson shook his head, negative. "Everyone heard the blast but Security was paying attention to outside the perimeter. The nearest personnel when it happened were me and Sergeant Hines and the Lieutenant."

Grey indicated his bandage. "I caught this when my patrol was ambushed the other night. I was laid up in my hooch, woozy on pain pills the medic gave me. But we compared notes. No one saw anything. It wasn't the VC. They'd never breach our perimeter."

Hines indicated the Tactical Operations command bunker.

"The captain and I were sprucing up the files for the

Inspector General's visit, day after tomorrow. If it hadn't been for a couple of walls between the colonel's hooch and the TOC, we'd have been hamburger too."

"Any ideas about who'd want the Colonel dead bad enough to frag him?"

Larson said, "Suspects?" The flint was cold in his eyes. "Yeah, I could think of a few."

Grey cleared his throat. "You might as well go ahead and tell him, Cap."

Kelly said, "Tell us what, Captain Larson?"

This got McGavin's goat.

"Not us, ma'am. Me." He spoke to the men. "I take it the colonel was not well-liked."

Hines chuckled. "I'll bet you're saying that just because someone fragged his ass to hell."

McGavin said, "Colonel Emmett was assigned here just last month. A new CO always shakes up a command to put his own brand on it. The troops never like it but it usually settles into mutual respect after a while."

Hines regarded the damaged hooch with no visible sign of emotion.

"You want a list of suspects, Major? You could start with every man on this base."

Grey stared at the ground as if looking at something far, far away. "Eight men who were stationed here went home yesterday in body bags."

"A platoon from Bravo company," said Captain Larson. "Ambushed. Heavy casualties."

"Wiped out by one of our own bombs," said Hines. His eyes kept shifting back to the jungle tree line. "The VC find our dud shells, rig them up and use them against us."

"Let me guess," said McGavin. "Saigon promised replacements today but they're not here."

Larson nodded. "The green machine. Efficient as hell, ain't it? And until those new men get here, I'm way short of manpower. I'm hoping Charlie hasn't figured that out yet."

"Issue me an M16," said McGavin. "You've got one replacement."

"Two, actually," Kelly volunteered.

They ignored her.

McGavin didn't miss the flash of anger that made Kelly's eyes turn a deeper shade of green.

He went around to the entrance of the command center and glanced inside. Tactical maps were spread out upon folding tables. Ammo crates served as chairs. A clerk was busy at a typewriter. A radioman monitored mostly static from a small receiver.

Grey said, "Colonel Emmett should never have ordered me and my men out on that patrol."

Larson told McGavin, "The firebase is assigned two companies of light infantry. One supports the other. The line company conducts recon patrols around the base and it was Bravo Company's turn on the rotation schedule. The other company provides mortar and artillery support from here."

"The colonel should have never ordered my platoon into that area after dark," said Grey. "I'm not some wet behind the ears cherry. That ambush wasn't my fault. Me and Sergeant Williams always brought our guys home. Right, Captain?

Larson nodded. "Right, Lieutenant."

Sergeant Hines said, not unkindly, "You need to chill out, Lieutenant, if you don't mind my saying so, sir. You, uh, haven't been right since, well, since it happened. Maybe you ought to lay down in your hooch, sir. I'll have a medic check in with you."

A sideways glance told McGavin that an impulse within Kelly was trying to dissuade her from capturing on film, for posterity, Lieutenant Grey's vulnerability and emotional unbalance—a poignant portrait of the ravages of war on a trained, competent man. She grimaced, lifted her camera and snapped the picture.

Grey said, "The sergeant who died in the ambush, Sergeant Williams, he served way back in the Korean war and, until two nights ago, he was keeping alive a good bunch of guys who should have been back home drinking beer. Every man on the base respected him. The sarge was our teacher, our preacher, the one we looked up to. And I owed him a personal debt. That's why I wish to God that *I'd* been one of the dead in that VC ambush, not him."

"Lieutenant," said Larson, "you are not responsible for what happened."

McGavin said, "What sort of personal debt?"

"My dad served with Sergeant Williams in Korea," said Grey. "He saved Dad's life. Sarge greased a Red Chinese who was about to run Dad through with a bayonet. They stayed in touch after the war. They were both lifers. I must have heard the story a hundred times growing up. I never got tired of it. Cancer got Dad last year. I was raised to be a soldier. I couldn't believe my luck when I got assigned to Sergeant Williams. I was supposed to be the platoon leader but we all knew who kept us alive." Grey's lower lip trembled.

Kelly stepped forward. She rested a hand gently on Grey's shoulder.

"Lieutenant, listen to your Captain and to Sergeant Hines. There is a thing called survivor's guilt. You must assert yourself. That is what you owe Sergeant Williams and your dad and yourself."

Grey's lower lip stopped trembling.

"Yes, ma'am. You're right." He drew himself to his full height, his shoulders back. "I'm not doing anybody any good, pissing and whining, am I? I've got to regroup and be ready for whatever's coming next."

Kelly nodded with a smile. "I couldn't have said it better myself."

Grey turned to Larson. "Captain, uh, I guess maybe I should try and get some rest."

"I think you're right, Lieutenant. You're dismissed."

"Thank you, sir." Grey added to Kelly, "And thank you, ma'am." He lowered his eyes from theirs and walked away.

When Grey was out of earshot, Larson said, "There goes a fine soldier, wearing a hair shirt from hell."

"He'll make it," said Hines. "That kid's got a lot to offer this man's army but he was on the razor's edge of losing it. Miss Carpenter, I believe you helped steer that soldier back in the right direction."

Kelly started to say something.

McGavin spoke before she could.

"Yes, ma'am. That was a humane and noble gesture. But now I will ask you to allow me to proceed without distraction. You're a non-participating observer, Miss Carpenter. Captain, let's take a look at Sergeant Williams' hooch."

"This way," said Larson. He started them toward a line of hooches near a row of mortar placements. "Mind if I ask, Major, what are we looking for in Williams' hooch?"

Striding apace with them, Kelly said, "The Lieutenant

said the men on the base looked up to Sergeant Williams like a hero."

Hines nodded. "That's as good a word as any, ma'am, and that's why everyone really hated the colonel after Sergeant Williams died on a patrol that never should have been sent out." A bleak smile creased his coffee latte features. "And that's the connection. I get it. Lady, you're a Sherlock Holmes."

McGavin tried hard not to yield to his building irritation.

He said, "She's a civilian." *This wasn't going to work, having Kelly tagging along every step of the way. He would just lay it all out when they got back to HQ. They had a war to win. He had a murder to solve. What the hell was Kelly thinking? What the hell was she doing here?* Cool it, he told himself. He said, "And I'll thank you, Miss Carpenter, to just zip it and take your pictures, okay?"

"Understood, General."

McGavin sighed. "Sarcasm yet. I'll be lucky to stay a major with you bird-dogging me." He barely caught the man-to-man grin that passed between Larson and the First Sergeant at this verbal sparring. Damn. The electricity between him and this sassy redhead was so obvious that anyone who witnessed it would catch on even if they didn't know exactly what they were seeing. To change the subject, he nodded to the row of mortars near Williams' hooch. "Not the quietest neighborhood."

"No such thing as a quiet neighborhood in this sector," said Hines. "We're surrounded by bogey land. It's a free-fire zone beyond that perimeter."

"The first change Colonel Emmett made when he took command," said Larson, "was to start sending out patrols after dark. It was unnecessary. Too risky. Everyone except the colonel knew it. The mission for this firebase is recon. You can't recon in the jungle at night."

Hines spat. "We have an outstanding record for targeting VC for the flyboys. We do our job. But doing our job wasn't good enough for the colonel, that is, as long as he didn't have to get off his fat ass in the TOC bunker. He wanted a higher enemy body count so he could get himself a general's star and he didn't give a damn about sacrificing good men like Sergeant Williams for a promotion."

Kelly lifted her camera and snapped a picture of Hines.

They reached Williams' hooch.

McGavin entered the hooch alone. Kelly lowered her camera and positioned herself between Hines and Larson in the entrance. Their grouped presence in the doorway deepened the interior gloom. The hooch was of uniform furnishings: cot, footlocker, a makeshift desk. McGavin knelt on one knee to conduct a thorough search of the footlocker.

"Uh *huh*," he said.

He rose, letting the lid of the locker snap shut. He exited the hooch, leafing through a small bound leather volume.

Captain Larson craned his neck to try to make out the printing on the book.

"What did you find, Major?"

Hines guessed, "A Bible?"

McGavin shook his head, snapping the book shut. "Not even close.

Kelly studied the book's dimensions and appearance. "A diary."

"When men keep one, it's called a journal."

Larson ran a broad palm across the bristle of his crewcut. "Why would Sergeant Williams keep a journal?"

"Why the hell wouldn't he?" growled Hines. "I'll bet he had plenty of stories to tell, going back to Korea."

"Too bad he kept them to himself." Larson extended his hand, palm up. "Mind if I take a look, Major? Maybe he wrote something that will help us."

Kelly said, "You could make a bet on that."

McGavin slid the book into a pocket. "Sorry. First, I'll have a look for myself."

Kelly studied him. "You think that diary—excuse me, journal—holds a clue to who fragged the colonel?"

"That's what I intend to find out." McGavin patted the book in his pocket. "Something tells me this is going to make for an interesting read and I want to get started."

Sergeant Hines said, "I'll show you to the guest billets, for what they're worth." He glanced at his watch. "And it's past chow time."

* * *

Kelly let herself into one of the guest billets—not her own—without announcing her arrival.

McGavin sat at a makeshift desk, a slab of plywood resting across two empty oil drums. Remaining seated, he pivoted with incredible speed, a blur of movement, freezing with the .45 in straight-armed target acquisition, its muzzle inches away from and aimed at the center of Kelly's forehead.

She froze, lovely mouth agape, her green eyes wide, holding her breath in astonishment.

McGavin sighed mightily, flicked on the safety and returned the .45 to its shoulder holster.

"Now there was a real temptation." He returned to the material spread across the desk. "I thought we were going to avoid personal contact, Miss Carpenter."

She stood beside him. She rested a hand on his shoulder. Her touch had always had its intended effect on him. He felt that humanizing affirmation borne of the touch of woman, of grace and beauty so uncommon, practically unknown in the harshness of war except as memories nursed by those who fought. She glimpsed the paperwork he'd been poring over: three personnel files, a yellow pad full of his notations and the slim leather volume, folded open with the spine up.

She read aloud the names off the personnel files.

"Captain Larson, Lieutenant Grey, Sergeant Hines. I'm glad I don't have to guess which one of those three fragged the colonel."

McGavin decided that he could either blow up or give up. This woman had a backbone of steel coupled with a tenacity that could wear down stone.

"And what makes you think the killer is one of them or that I'm guessing? It's called investigating. What the hell am I going to do with you?"

An impish smile curved her lips, and with one graceful, impudent motion she was straddling his lap, her fingers entwined behind his neck, mischievous green eyes glistening, her lips, inviting, only inches away.

She whispered huskily in his ear, "I've got an idea what you could do with me."

"You're a vexatious wench."

"Vexatious?"

"Sometimes I wish you were more of a nag. That would be easier to deal with."

Realizing that he was serious, she lost some of her good humor. She withdrew from his lap.

"So, what about the journal? Was it interesting?"

"What journal?"

At that instant, someone outside yelled, *"Incoming!"*

Then everything became drowned out by a startling, eerie whistling that increased in pitch and then was itself drowned out by a deafening explosion, an impacting blast that shook the hooch violently. Dust and red dirt powdered down upon them.

McGavin grabbed the M16 he'd been issued and had propped against the bunk. He rushed outside.

A night fog had fallen. A bursting flare overhead cast the base in surreal daylight. The first explosion had been a direct hit on the Huey that had brought them here, now nothing but an unrecognizable, flaming ruin. Everywhere on the base, soldiers were responding to the attack, some firing their M16's on the run, firing the weapons on full auto into the darkness beyond the perimeter. The artillery and the mortars and machine guns opened up, shredding the night with thunder and fury.

A whistling round missed McGavin by inches, chipping off a chunk of the hooch doorframe. He felt a trickle of blood from a flying splinter, razor-thin along his cheek.

The next incoming mortar shell struck the main bunker. The Tactical Operations Command evaporated in a copper-red eruption of flame.

Then Kelly was with him.

She said, "Damn but I wish they'd issued me a weapon. Don't suppose I could borrow one of yours?"

McGavin grabbed her wrist. "First, let's get you to cover. They're targeting the hooches."

They stormed into the battle, dodging strobe-like explosions. Shouts filled the air along with the stench of destruction, of burnt gunpowder, of dying and killing. McGavin led her to a nearby pile of debris somewhat in the shadows of empty oil drums and discarded machine parts. It was a good place to stash a troublesome wife until the fighting was over. A round pinged off an overhanging piece of metal. She was right. He could not leave her unarmed.

He handed her his M16. "Here. You qualified with one of these on the range back home. Time for practical application. Keep your head down. You are a non-combatant." He unleathered the .45 from its shoulder holster and flicked off the safety. "I've got to keep moving, to help out."

She took hold of the rifle, wholly comfortable with it. Then her eyes were distracted by something.

"Cord, look."

He whirled, half knowing what to expect. Then he saw it too.

Through the disorganized melee of battle, a soldier, whose features were obscured, darted through the tumultuous firefight with determined haste, staying low to avoid incoming fire, one hand steadying his helmet as he ran, appearing to McGavin to be somehow disengaged from the battle, particularly when he gained the hooch the McGavins had just vacated. The soldier entered the guest billet.

"Wait here," said McGavin and he bolted.

"Right," Kelly said to herself.

She gave McGavin a ten count, then she slung the M16 over her shoulder by its strap and followed him.

* * *

McGavin hesitated at the entrance to the hooch, the .45 automatic held down at his side, his presence undetected by the man inside because of the ferocious battle raging around them and because the soldier was preoccupied, in the process of reaching for the slim black book on the desk.

McGavin said, "It's not a journal."

Larson whirled. His expression struggled between surprise and panic.

"Major, I can explain."

They had to raise their voices to be heard above the cacophony outside.

"Captain, I'm arresting you," said McGavin. "You murdered Colonel Emmett. You fragged a fellow officer."

Larson drew his broad, farmer's body up straight, doing his best to reassert command even if he was outranked.

"Arrest me? On the strength of what? Every man on this base wanted to see that bastard dead."

"Yeah, but you're the one who went for the bait." McGavin nodded to the black book. "That's no journal. It's a notebook that I always carry. I had it on me when I knelt down to search Williams' footlocker and with the dim lighting inside the hooch and a little sleight of hand I had everyone thinking I'd found it there in the footlocker. I wanted to see if I could smoke out someone with a guilty conscience and it looks like I succeeded."

"Bullshit, Major," sneered Larson. "You're making this up as you go along."

McGavin pressed on with not a shred of doubt in his

voice.

"Let me guess. Discontent and the notion of frag-ging the colonel had been whispered around this base since before Sergeant Williams and Lieutenant Grey took out that patrol two nights ago. You and the late sergeant even discussed it between the two you, man to man. A solder like Sergeant Williams would have told you to bite your tongue and follow orders. After you thought I'd found a journal, you got worried that Williams might have made note of that conversation in it. That is, if he'd kept a journal."

The sneer was gone. Larson licked his dry lips.

"You've got me all wrong, Major."

"I don't think so," said McGavin. "You wanted to see if Williams incriminated you. Maybe I hadn't gotten to that page yet and you could steal the book before I did. A crazy long shot but it was the only chance you saw so you went for it."

A sudden jolt of raw, bitter emotion erupted from Larson.

"That's exactly what he told me. Let it alone, he said. Follow orders. Right, follow orders. Sounds real honorable, don't it? But look what it got the sarge and those men of Bravo Company. That fucking Emmett was killing my men, goddammit. He *had* to be stopped and I stopped him!"

A shell struck the next hooch over with a thunderous *crack!* like a lightning strike. Shouts for *"Medic! Medic!"* could be heard.

Larson lunged at McGavin. *"Bastard!"*

McGavin had hoped that sight of the .45 would dis-courage something like this but Larson wasn't about to be taken easily. He could escape into the jungle or die trying.

McGavin brought up the .45.

The *snap!* of a camera flashbulb came from close behind his ear.

Kelly had crept up from outside and eavesdropped. The white flash seared the interior of the hooch, not impairing McGavin's vision because it came from behind him. The flash startled, stunned and stopped Larson. He reflexively threw his arms up to cover his eyes.

Kelly said, "Gotcha!"

McGavin brought his .45 around in a swipe that cracked the side of Larson's head. Larson's knees buckled and he collapsed. McGavin pinned him with a boot to Larson's back. He holstered the .45 and reached for the handcuffs attached to his belt. He spared a quick glance over his shoulder.

The beauty of her model's face was smudged with grime. Her red hair was tangled. She looked stunning.

He said, "Thanks, hon."

Larson's face, against the earthen floor, was an emotionless mask.

"You've got this all wrong, Major. Yeah, I thought it was Williams' journal that you found. I came for a look to see if he thought anyone on base killed Emmett, to see if he wrote that down. I didn't frag anybody."

"Sergeant Hines will fess up," said McGavin. "He gave you your alibi when he said you and he were together prepping for the IG inspection. But Sergeant Hines is lying because he hated Emmett too. You weren't in the TOC bunker with your First Sergeant when Emmett was killed. I'll go to work on Top's conscience and his duty under the Uniform Code of Military Justice and when he breaks, Captain, I'll have the proof I need."

Larson sneered. "What the hell kind of a soldier are you? Whose side are you on, McGavin? I'm on the side of *our* troops. That's more important than any VC body count so some fat-assed colonel can advance his career. You think I could let that go on? *Our* body count is my concern. Let me go. Emmett got what he deserved. You know that, in your heart."

"You're out of luck, Captain. It's my job to take you in."

Someone outside yelled, *"Incoming!"* and again the air was split by that fast-approaching, ear-piercing whistle.

McGavin sprang at Kelly without hesitation, yelling to the man on the floor, "Move, Larson! Save yourself!

Larson got to his feet but made no effort to leave.

He said in a calm voice, "Up yours, Major."

With the incoming whistle growing impossibly loud, McGavin plowed into Kelly with enough force to knock her off her feet, sending them both airborne, pitching them outside of the hooch and onto ground. They landed together. Cord's arms were around her. They rolled a few times before coming to a stop with Cord on top.

Again, lightning and thunder struck. The ground trembled beneath them as a direct hit demolished the hooch. McGavin pinned his wife, shielding her from a pelting shower of falling debris.

Then they lifted their heads.

The battle was winding down. Three Huey gunships had motored in to commence pulverizing the surrounding jungle, making the night sky a fire show of tracer bullets, rocket fire and multiple explosions. There was no more incoming fire. The mortars and artillery were quieting down. The primary activity on the base now was tending to the wounded, regrouping, assessing.

Kelly arched her neck for a view of the smoldering remains of the hooch they had just vacated.

"Captain Larson..."

"It's better this way," said McGavin. "He died in combat. That's better for his family back in the world."

"You're not going to report that he fragged a colonel?"

McGavin said nothing.

She stared up at him for a long moment. Then she kissed the thin red line of dried blood that crossed his cheek and, for one stolen moment, there on the battle-scarred ground, they shared a prolonged embrace.

"Know what?' whispered Kelly.

"What?"

"It's been so long, I wouldn't even mind being on the bottom."

"You," said McGavin, "are impossible."

"And that's only one of the reasons you're crazy about me, right?"

"Yeah, I guess so. Crazy is definitely the word. I must be out of my mind." Two figures were hurrying in their direction. "Here come Sergeant Hines and Lieutenant Grey. I've got some explaining to do." He got up off her, extending a courtly hand. Kelly accepted, rising to her feet, and he said for her ears alone, "Now stow the personal stuff, okay, hon? I mean it, Kelly. For real."

He turned to greet the approaching men.

"Right," Kelly said to herself and hurried to join them.

Chez Erotique

....

(short story)

Kelly wanted to try a new position from the *Kama Sutra.*
But after thirty minutes, the sexual heat between her and
McGavin built to such a sweat-drenched, panting intensity that they decided the hell with the *Kama Sutra* and
switched to that good old serviceable missionary position.

Bedsprings rocked. Sheets became hot and tangled.

The telephone rang.

McGavin said, "Sorry, hon."

They were in the bedroom of his private living quarters. He was supposed to be off duty.

Kelly reluctantly unlocked her ankles.

"But sweetie, it's 0200." Kelly was not the pouting type.
At the moment, it gave her a sultry look. "Can't you—"

"Unfortunately, this is the time of day when my work
happens," said McGavin.

He picked up the receiver and spoke his name.

A male voice replied, speaking precise English with a Viet accent.

"Forgive me, Major. I am most sorry to bother you at this hour. Your man, Sergeant Samuels—"

McGavin recognized the voice.

"Not as sorry as I am, Captain. What's up?"

Captain Pham was an investigator for the Army of the Republic of Vietnam's criminal investigation Saigon detachment. They had worked cases together when US military and ARVN interests intersected. Their current joint US/ARVN undertaking was an undercover investigation into the city's extensive black market operations. Pham had proven himself to be a man of intelligence and honesty.

Honesty, of course, being relative these days in Saigon with plenty of gray areas. Since Pham was exemplary in performing his investigative duties whenever they worked together, McGavin allowed himself to remain neutral upon learning early in their association that the dapper, good-natured ARVN officer also happened to be a part-owner of an exclusive sex club, *Chez Erotique*, in the city's red-light district.

Pham said, "We have a serious problem, you and I. Big trouble."

McGavin swung himself to sit up on the edge of the bed. He became aware of Kelly's stroking fingers. With a reproving glare, he brushed the fingers away and forced himself to remain focused.

He said, "Are we talking about Mr. Smith?"

"Frankly, Major," said Pham, "my hope is that you will be the one to determine that."

Mr. Smith, which everyone understood to be a cover name, was said to be a shaper and mover of the black market underground. Mr. Smith was an elusive, seemingly omnipotent underworld presence. One word from Mr. Smith and people died. Yet his identity remained a mystery.

"Okay," said McGavin, "let's hear it."

Pham said, "It's about your man Samuels—"

"Not my man," McGavin interrupted. "The sergeant is an informant. He's a rotten soldier. He's working a deal he cut after I busted him."

"He is dead," said Pham. "He has been murdered."

"Then we are talking Mr. Smith."

"That is most likely. I, uh, regret to say the sergeant was murdered at *Chez Erotique*. I am calling from there now. I have just arrived. I thought it best to contact you immediately. Given my association with this business, you see, it could prove, er, problematic at a number of levels."

"You thought right," said McGavin. "Okay, you owe me one. Get out of there. I'll head down there and do what I can."

"I am most grateful, Major." Pham sounded genuinely and profoundly relieved.

"Our investigation is undercover," said McGavin. "Let's keep it that way, at least for a few more hours."

"That would be most beneficial. Thank you, Major."

"This conversation isn't taking place," said McGavin. "You aren't there."

"I see. I understand."

"I'm on my way down. Samuels is . . . was an American soldier. You're not involved. I'll try to pick up whatever lead Samuels was following. Unless, of course, he was bullshitting me and he didn't go there following a lead, like he told me. Could be he just wanted a quickie. I'll share with you whatever I learn."

"As you say," said Pham, "I owe you one. The woman who manages the establishment for me, her name is Tran Le. I trust her. Again, thank you, Major. Thank you very much."

And the phone connection went dead.

McGavin replaced the receiver. He reached for a casual shirt and jeans on a nearby chair.

Kelly left the bed, a vision of nude perfection. She emerged from the bathroom a few minutes later, having hurriedly thrown on the blue-dotted white summer dress she'd worn on their dinner date. In heels and with a modest neckline of the dress, she managed to somehow look wholesome and sexy at the same time.

She said in a voice that matched her appearance, "Where to, Major?"

"Where do you think? I'm taking you home. I've got work to do."

McGavin was fully dressed and ready to go. A lightweight sports jacket concealed the shoulder holstered Army-issue Colt .45 that he habitually wore under his left arm.

"So, we've got another case?"

"Not we. Me. I said I'm taking you home."

"Now you're not being nice at all. You know I won't get in the way."

"I know no such thing and I'm going someplace you've never been."

"Try me."

McGavin sighed.

They left his quarters together. With time now of the

essence, he mentally reassessed this situation. He decided to relent, hoping he wouldn't regret it. McGavin allowed Kelly to accompany him on his drive into the heart of the city.

On its surface, life in Saigon could seem to be mostly unscathed by much direct violence of the war. There was the random, occasional urban guerilla action by the Vietcong but the boulevards and streets were lively. Even now, in the middle of the night, the main thoroughfares were clogged with cars, trucks, trishaws, pedicabs and countless bicycles. Itinerate vendors wandered in hordes, shrilly hawking their wares.

As his '67 Pontiac negotiated the maze, McGavin told Kelly about Captain Pham, about what a good investigator Pham was, and of Pham's part-ownership of a sex club. Kelly listened without comment.

"I busted Samuels," McGavin told her. "He was diverting merchandise from the Post Exchange and the NCO Club, pulling down a profit selling everything from nylons to beer to transistor radios for top dollar to Viet civilians. He got mean with a bookkeeper at the PX who wouldn't look the other way and the bookkeeper came to CID. We've been using Samuels to try and get a lead on the next link up in the black market chain." McGavin briefly explained the mystery of Mr. Smith's identity. "Tonight, Samuels thought he was getting close. At least that's what he told me this afternoon, the last time we made contact."

Kelly considered what she'd heard.

"So, tonight the sergeant was getting close to Mr. Smith and tonight he's murdered in a swanky sex club. Coincidence?"

"Don't believe in 'em," said McGavin. "When I find

who killed Samuels, maybe I'll have Mr. Smith."

"*We* will have him, darling," Kelly said sweetly.

McGavin concentrated on his driving.

Chez Erotique was a well-kept, three-story house set back from the street. Its ornate ironwork around the windows was an elegant holdover from the days of French colonialism. Such a sedate, upscale bordello was a world apart from the gaudy neon fleshpots surrounding it. Far from being a bump-and-grind sweathouse for over-heated infantrymen, it was a classy establishment for those who could afford it, priced to keep out the riff-raff—a place where discriminating gentlemen from the American and Viet military and the private sector could discreetly indulge their pleasures with, it was said, the prettiest working girls in Saigon.

The interior was comfortably air-conditioned, designed to lull and appeal to the senses. Muted traditional Vietnamese music wafted through the air as did the scent of lavender incense. The furnishings were plush with many pillows. The lighting was soft, indirect.

And yet, when the madam, Tran Le, awaiting their arrival, met them at the front door and showed them to the death room, McGavin sensed a musky, cloying aura of sex about the place, despite the incense. It seemed to emanate from every wall as if these walls had, over the years, absorbed the essence of the endless carnal activity that went on here.

Tran Le was Eurasian. Mid-thirties. Too old to be a working girl, she embodied a ripened, mature feminine allure. Her jet-black hair was pinned up elegantly. A low-cut something of clinging material accentuated her curves. A shawl of pale blue silk draped bare shoulders and arms.

Pham had prepared her for their arrival. She had first checked McGavin's military ID before allowing them admittance. McGavin introduced Kelly with a simple, "This is Miss Carpenter," and provided no further information. That was fine with Tran Le whose demeanor was calm to the point of serenity even as she guided them down a hallway and up a flight of stairs.

In a second-floor bedroom, the corpse was sprawled across the rumpled sheets of an antique iron bed. Beyond one wall, in the next room, rocking bedsprings and enthusiastic lovemaking could be faintly heard. The dead man was Caucasian with a military buzz cut. Slacks and underwear gathered around his knees. A knife was rammed to the hilt into his lower back, beneath the bottom left rib.

Kelly and the madam remained near the closed door, observing McGavin as he stood registering his first impressions of the scene.

Kelly said to Tran Le, almost as if making idle conversation with the hint of a smile, "This is the real death, no? I don't suppose your establishment is any stranger to the Little Death as our French friends call the orgasm?"

The madam nodded.

"*Le petite morte.* It is the reason *Chez Erotique* exists."

Kelly indicated the corpse on the bed.

"Is this the first homicide committed here?"

"This has never happened here before," said Tran Le. She has a throaty voice and a pronounced French accent. "As a matter of fact," she added, "the house prides itself on our security measures."

McGavin said, "He wasn't supposed to be here. This place is off-limits to US Army personnel."

Tran Le smiled.

"Men are wont to go wherever they wish and do whatever they wish, regardless of rules and regulations, if the urge is strong enough. Is that not so?"

It was a rhetorical question.

Kelly cleared her throat. She had not missed McGavin's visual inventory of Tran Le, nor the obvious charms of this alluring woman. *Great,* thought McGavin. *I'm dealing with a homicide and the wife is about to get jealous in a whorehouse.* But Kelly surprised him. She indicated the body on the bed.

"Has he been dead long?"

There was only the slightest trace of cattiness in her tone.

McGavin said, "I'm no medical examiner. And may I remind you, Miss Carpenter, that your newspaper assignment in-country, as I understand it, is to accompany me as a photojournalist, *not* help me solve crimes."

Tran Le heard words she did not like. She frowned.

"Photo? Newspaper? But there can be no photographs. This is not a respectable business but we are discreet."

Kelly said, "Don't worry, hon. I'm not here to take pictures. I was visiting the major when you called."

She did place minor emphasis on the word *visiting*, suggestive enough for Tran Le to get the message. Beyond that, Kelly appeared satisfied that something she'd said had gotten under the woman's skin and that she'd established her turf.

Tran Le said to McGavin, "He paid for this room and one of my girls. She ran to me screaming and I came here and found him like that. I searched his wallet for ID. When I see that he is a serviceman, I immediately called Captain Pham."

McGavin nodded.

"And he called me. Was this man one of your regular patrons?"

Tran Le sniffed. An elegant sniff of distaste.

"Most certainly not. The average enlisted man can hardly afford *Chez Erotique.* I have never seen this man before. Pham said that you could help. Can this be kept from any official report? Can the body be moved?"

McGavin dodged the question.

"How quiet has this been kept so far?"

The lovemaking sounds from the next room had intensified.

"I told you," said Tran Le. "The girl he was with came straight to me. She was hysterical. In shock."

Kelly asked, before McGavin had the chance, "Could the girl have done it? Maybe he was carrying a bankroll and she—"

"She is a good girl," Tran Le said as if that settled that.

"I'll want to talk with this girl," said McGavin. "What did she say happened?"

"She was hysterical. She could offer nothing, only that Samuels wanted the lights off. He wanted them in darkness. Then . . . it happened suddenly. Someone burst in. She claims to have seen nothing."

He returned his attention to the body on the bed.

"The blade pierced his heart. He died instantly."

Blood had seeped from around the knife and was partly congealed on the sheet beneath to the body. McGavin removed the coverlet from the foot of the bed and spread the sheet across Samuels' body.

Tran Le said, "And so you will help, Major, to, uh, clear this up, is that the saying?"

"That's it," said McGavin. "So, no one knows about this yet except you, Captain Pham and the girl who was in here with Samuels?"

"Yes, that is correct."

"Okay, take me to the girl. I need to talk to her."

Tran Le's smile was contrite.

"I regret to say that after Captain Pham left here, there were complications."

"What sort of complications?"

"The girl was hysterical as I've said. I'm afraid . . . she's gone."

"Gone?"

"She was left unattended for but an instant and she ran screaming into the night. At this moment, I am sorry to say that I have no idea where she is. But I have taken steps to see that she is returned."

"What sort of steps?"

"My security manager—"

"You mean your bouncer."

Tran Le's bosom moved with a sigh beneath the pale blue shawl.

"As you like. His name is Ky. He is most formidable in these matters and he knows every inch of Little Texas. I have sent him after her. She will not escape from Ky. He will return with her within the next half hour, of that I am certain."

"Captain Pham is aware of this?"

"He is. Given the circumstances here and the fact that this," she indicated Samuels' body without actually looking at it, "will be—shall I say—privately handled, the captain felt it would be best if the girl chooses not to return though, frankly, I believe she will if Ky does not locate her first. The captain asked me to extend his apologies and begs your indulgence."

Eyeing McGavin for his reaction, Kelly said, "Your ARVN friend seems to need plenty of that, doesn't he, Major? Your indulgence, I mean."

"I told Pham I'd cover this," said McCord, "and I will. I can pull strings to keep this off the morning report and out of the *Stars & Stripes* but I do intend to find out what Samuels knew before someone killed him."

Kelly said, "Suspect number one has to be the missing girl, good girl or not, right? She sticks a knife in the guy and runs with money she took from his wallet."

"Could have happened that way," McGavin conceded. "Tran Le, I'll cut your man another fifteen minutes to turn her up. The only reason I'm cutting you slack is that she might have something that will help me and Pham with our black market investigation."

"I know of this investigation," said Tran Le. "You and Pham must be most careful, sir. The man they call Mr. Smith, whoever he may be, he is very dangerous." She again indicated the corpse without looking at it. "This is proof, *non*?"

"Fifteen minutes," McCord repeated. "After that, I call it in and do what I can. Samuels wasn't much of a soldier but his body deserves some respect."

Kelly said, "You are so *damn* sensitive, Major."

The lovemaking next door had finally quieted down to nothing.

"And during those fifteen minutes," said Tran Le in a quiet voice, "perhaps, Major, you and the lady would care to relax here at *Chez Erotique*. There are the occasional couples who choose to avail themselves, you may be surprised to learn."

McGavin noted that, as with the corpse, the madam indicated Kelly without actually casting a glance at her.

Women, thought McGavin again.

But Kelly would not be denied.

"And how," she asked, "would a couple go about spending those fifteen minutes?"

Tran Le said, "I would suggest the viewing of one of our private shows. Couples or singles may watch erotic performances from their personal, private booth." She glanced at the watch on her slim wrist. "A show is scheduled to begin shortly. What do you say?" She did appraise Kelly this time, arching a thin eyebrow. "Would you care to indulge?"

McGavin said, "Seems like a hell of a way to conduct a murder investigation."

Kelly nudged him with an elbow. Her green eyes danced.

"Major, that hysterical prostitute could provide a real lead. Fifteen minutes. Waiting is waiting. Come on, we haven't seen a good sex show in, oh, what's it been now, at least an hour?"

McGavin bristled.

"Miss Carpenter—" he started to say.

But Tran Le was already smoothly shifting gears, adroitly guiding Kelly by an elbow out of the room in a friendly, familiar manner.

He left the room, stepping into the corridor, closing the door behind him to rejoin his wife and Tran Le. The two women now appeared to be getting along like old friends, chatting in discreetly lowered voices with an occasional knowing smile passing between them.

The hallway ran the length of the building's second

story and was lined with closed doors. From behind those closed doors came sounds of lovemaking. A man happened out of one room with a hooker on each arm, strolling toward the stairway that led to the brothel's downstairs club area. From behind another door came a man's gravelly voice pleading hoarsely, followed by harsh feminine denial and the crack of a whip. From behind another door, the sounds of two women making torrid love. A door opened and a whore watched her john hurry away, the fellow looking guilty as sin.

The girls working the house were all young Vietnamese, dressed uniformly in high heels that jutted out butt and boobs, shapely legs encased in colored thigh-high nylons, the finishing touch being a shawl, similar to Madam's, artistically gilding the shapely, available human merchandise.

Tran Le had paused with Kelly next to a curtained archway. When McGavin reached them, Kelly greeted him with that mischievous glint in her eye.

"Tran Le was telling me what we're about to see."

The madam flashed McGavin a smile.

"I hope, Major, that you are not easily shocked."

"Not by sex," said McGavin. "It's the other things people do to each other that gets to me."

"I understand. Again, I thank you for your patience, truly. This way if you please."

McGavin decided, *Aw, what the hell.*

They stepped beyond the curtain, into a narrow corridor off the hallway that curved to the left where it widened into a dimly-lit area of closed doors. Tran Le opened the nearest door. They entered a compact room, more of a booth, also dimly lit. A black leather couch faced a window that comprised the upper half of one wall. Beyond the glass was soft lighting. Pink hues. No furniture. A small dais and a row of opaque windows, matching the one of this booth, lined the walls around the dais.

"One-way glass," McGavin observed.

"We guarantee our patrons absolute privacy to engage in whatever pleasures they wish," said Tran Le. "Is there anything else I can do for you?"

"No thanks," said Kelly. "We'll just pretend we're customers for a little while, right, Major?"

McGavin grumbled, "Customers trying to solve a murder."

"If you'll excuse me," said Tran Le.

With a nod to each, she left them.

When the door latched behind her, McGavin tried its handle. The door opened easily. He reclosed it, fighting the urge to unholster his .45. Kelly eyed his every move, intuitively reading him as she always did.

"I know, Cord. But I don't think us being brought back here is a trap. Whoever killed the sergeant is long gone by now, don't you think?"

McGavin turned from the door. He abruptly slid an arm around her waist. Yanking her to him, he commenced nuzzling her left ear.

Kelly emitted a surprised gasp.

"Oh, Major."

He whispered, "I'm thinking this booth is bugged."

Her hands clasped behind at his neck.

"So what?" she whispered in his ear. "I hope Tran Le isn't your killer. I like her."

McGavin growled, "I'd like to put you on the next plane back to the States. I must have been out of my mind from the start, going along with this nutty charade of yours."

"We're both crazy, darling. Happily, about each other. But let's talk about your friend, Captain Pham. Exactly how far do you trust him, really?"

McGavin sighed. Kelly's tenacity was a force of nature. It was one of the things he loved about her. He also loved the way her figure felt in his arms. The fragrance of her aroused his senses. The fact that this was a bogus clinch, intended to allow him to communicate with her in case the booth was bugged, could not diminish the sensation of her breasts and hips pressing against him. Their lovemaking had gone uncompleted when they'd been interrupted by Pham's phone call. Now, with Kelly in his arms, that sexual heat was close to reigniting.

He said, "Show's about to start."

He rotated her around in his arms, without releasing his embrace, so they could both watch through the one-way window.

The lilting Vietnamese music that was being piped throughout the house faded, to be replaced by subtle American jazz with a strong bass line and backbeat. In syncopation to this beat, two dancers—one male, one female—stepped onto the dais.

The male was muscular, taller than the average Vietnamese male, clad only in a skimpy loincloth.

The girl embodied the classic beauty of Vietnamese womanhood. Slim with a well-toned litheness. Black hair worn stylishly short framed high cheekbones, lush lips and sensual eyes. High heels. White nylons. Hips encased in a bikini bottom. Above that, she wore only a shawl and a smile.

The shawl was identical to those worn by the other girls working here, with the only difference being the madam's shawl which had been pale in color while the others, including that of this dancer, sported an oriental pattern, bright and shimmering.

Light artificial fog swirled in from an unseen smoke machine, licking the floor and walls, lending the artfully lit dais a dream-like quality. The dancers faced each other, swaying. The girl's shoulders shimmied gently, gracefully, her feminine roundness accentuated by the artfully draped shawl.

The dancers turned from each other to perform side by side, directly before each of the one-way windows, undulating to the beat of the music. Eyes closed in some private fantasy. Erotically caressing themselves intimately. Then they engaged in a steamy embrace. Lips met in an extended tongue kiss. One of the young man's hands slid beneath the shawl to cup an unseen breast. The girl leaned her head back, eyes closed, mouthing an unheard moan.

The pulse of the music intensified.

In the booth, as McGavin stood there his arms around Kelly, both of them watching the performance, he became aware of the subtle twitch and steady grinding of his wife's butt against the front of his slacks. Kelly slid her hands down to clasp each of his.

"Oh baby," she said softly.

On the dais, the male tightened his embrace. The girl swayed. The shawl dropped to become a luminous pool at her feet. Curls of artificial smoke partially obscured the entwined couple. He drew her to him and she came willingly. A dance less than coitus, more than suggestive . . .

But McGavin found himself unable to stop looking at the luminous pool of the dancer's discarded shawl. Something elusive nibbled at his subconscious, an irritation yearning to be acknowledged. And then his conscious mind got it.

Kelly sensed something. She turned in his arms to face him.

"Honey, what is it?"

He released her, already turning to swing open the booth door. Striding out.

He said, "I just thought of something."

Reality was intruding on the heat that had distracted Kelly.

She sighed. "Sorry, hon. Those dancers . . . uh, guess they got your wife going for a second there. Guess they got my brain a little steamed up."

"Brain?"

"Well, part of me anyway. Uh, guess I'm not that good when it comes to self-discipline, huh?"

"You're not much good for my self-control either," McGavin muttered. "It's why I don't like having you around."

The second-floor corridor was clear of personnel. Voices carried up from the lounge area. McGavin stalked in that direction. Kelly hurried to keep up right behind him.

They met a man coming up the stairs. A Viet civilian. Stocky, wearing creased slacks, a loud Hawaiian shirt and a pistol holstered at his hip. The house security man, most likely moonlighting ARVN or police.

The guy said, "I am Ky. You are McGavin?"

McGavin nodded. "Did you find the girl?"

"I did." Ky led them down the stairs. "I have just returned. Tran Le sent me to get you."

At the bottom of the stairs, he led them across a dimly lit club area that was furnished with plush couches and a bar with an effeminate male bartender. Ky led them un-

obtrusively through a small cluster of young, provocatively dressed working girls who mingled with male customers, socializing as the customers made their selection.

McGavin and Kelly accompanied Ky through a swing
door in a dark corner. McGavin's fingertips stayed near
the butt of the concealed .45. Kelly followed him closely.
They'd entered a woman's lounge where the girls of *Chez
Erotique* could withdraw to freshen up. A row of stalls
faced a row of mirrors and porcelain.

The disheveled young prostitute cowered, biting her
lower lip and trembling, regarding them with wide, fearful
eyes. No more than a teenager despite the rouge, heels
and camisole. She'd lost her "uniform" shawl somewhere
along the way. She wasn't struggling, obviously intimidat-
ed. Tran Le was holding onto each of the girl's wrists as
she spoke, her tone alternating, argumentative, between
stern recrimination and persuasion.

Ky hovered, watching. Kelly stayed at McGavin's side.

The madam finally released the girl's wrists.

"This is the one who fled, Major." She rearranged
her pale shawl that had slid down in disarray about her
bare arms and shoulders. The shawl's Asian print again
reminded McGavin of the brighter, otherwise identical
shawls worn by the dancer and the other working girls
of this house. She went on, "You see the shape the poor
child is in. She denies killing your soldier, of course. But
I was wrong about her. I see that now. No one else could
have done it. She had motive and opportunity, no? She
killed Sergeant Samuels for the money in his wallet.
Then she panicked and fled into the night. Murder is
not for everyone."

The prostitute wailed.

"I no kill anyone! I good fuck girl! Sergeant, he fuck me. Lights go out. Someone come in and attack sergeant. Everything happen fast in dark. Then quiet. I turn on light. Sergeant is *dead!* Killer gone! I *good* fuck girl. *I no killer!*"

McGavin leaned down and took gentle hold of the girl gently by each elbow. She cringed away from him at first until she realized he was guiding her toward Kelly, who saw something in McGavin's expression that prompted her to place a comforting arm protectively around the young woman's waist.

McGavin said to Tran Le, "The girl performing in that peep show you steered us to was wearing a shawl identical to yours. Same print and everything. Except for one thing. The shawl you're wearing is pale. Hers was bright. That bugged me down in my subconscious. Then I got it. Your shawl is exactly like the others . . . *except you're wearing yours inside out.* That got me wondering why."

Her eyes narrowed.

"Stay away from me, Major."

He reached out and snatched the shawl from her before she could react. He held up the shawl.

Smeared blood on its inverse side was clearly visible.

McGavin said, "You were concealing these bloodstains that you picked up when you turned off the lights in that bedroom and stuck a knife into the sergeant's back. You couldn't get rid of the shawl, I guess. It's part of your standard apparel and you didn't want to draw attention to yourself once the girl turned on the lights and started raising a ruckus a few seconds later. You simply reversed the shawl and wore it inside out to conceal the bloodstains until you could dispose of it without arousing suspicion."

Tran Le drew herself erect. Her aristocratic features became haughty and aloof.

"That is a quite ridiculous charge. Yesterday one of the girls accidentally injured herself. That is how these bloodstains—"

"Stop it, Tran Le," said McGavin. "You killed the sergeant."

At his side, her arm remaining secure around the young girl, Kelly was frowning.

"But Cord, *why* would Tran Le kill Samuels?"

Tran Le scrutinized McGavin venomously.

"Yes, Major." Her words dripped venom. "What was my motive?"

"The only motive that would justify you murdering him on the spot without planning," said McGavin. "Tran Le, he pegged *you* as Mr. Smith. He told me he was closing in and he came here. Captain Pham isn't involved or he wouldn't have been asked me to come here in the first place. Instead of coming to me with the information like he was supposed to, Samuels tried to sell you his silence. That's the kind of weasel he was and that was real stupid of him because you shut him up permanently. You could have had your enforcer, Ky, do the killing, but those bloodstains tell me that this was important enough for you to want to deal with it yourself and so you did."

Ky sneered from where he remained holding up a wall.

"American, you talk shit. Where is your proof?"

"Forensics will match up the stains on Tran Le's shawl with the blood of Sergeant Samuels," said McGavin. "And that, dragon lady, is the end for you. You should've stayed with the black market and left murder alone."

Tran Le hissed like an angry snake. There was a flash

of tanned, perfectly shaped thigh with a garter that held a knife matching the knife that had protruded from Sergeant Samuels. This knife seemed to leap into Tran Le's hand.

"Ky!" she snarled.

A startled gasp from Kelly. A wail of despair from the prostitute.

Tran Le lunged for McGavin's throat with the skill of a street fighter. Ky plunged in, reaching for his sidearm. They came at McGavin from both sides.

He snap-kicked the knife from Tran Le's hand, sending it clattering to the floor. She hissed again, spun and took off darting for the lounge exit. McGavin couldn't give chase because by then Ky was on at him, his pistol clearing leather.

In a lightning-fast cross-draw, McGavin's .45 left its concealed holster, the automatic swinging outward in a stiff-armed arc, the barrel smacking Ky sharply upside his head. Ky toppled to the floor, unconscious.

At the same time, Kelly ran after Tran Le. She tackled Tran Le in a flying dive. Both women went hurtling to the floor just short of the door. Holstering his .45, McGavin stepped over to them. He produced stainless steel handcuffs from a pocket.

Kelly rolled free. McGavin cuffed Tran Le's wrists behind her back before the madam could regain her balance.

McGavin assisted Tran Le to her feet. She did not resist but she was swearing at him quietly, vehemently, alternating between sewer English, French and Vietnamese.

Kelly returned to the young prostitute who had been watching everything with uncertain eyes and a partially open mouth. Kelly led the girl to a couch. The girl sank down upon it, trembling less than before. She looked like a frightened child in whore's clothing.

"I good fuck girl. Men like! I no kill! I *good* fuck girl." Her terrified eyes flashed to Tran Le. "Why she say I kill man? I not murder anybody! *Why?*"

She again broke down into uncontrollable sobbing. Kelly sat beside her, embracing the woman-child like an older sister with gentle, cooing, comforting sounds that had a calming effect. The girl lowered her face to Kelly's shoulder. Her sobbing became more subdued.

Kelly caught McGavin's eye and said, "I'm willing to bet, Major, that you have an answer for the young lady."

"Once Tran Le knew I was looking for a connection between Samuels' murder and Mr. Smith, she decided to provide a fall guy for Samuels' murder and this girl was it. She was made to order."

Kelly glared at Tran Le.

"I've changed my mind, Cord. I don't like this bitch at all. And I guess I'm not much of a detective."

"No," he conceded, "but you are hell on wheels in a peep show and there's something to be said for that."

Sitting there, caring for a young woman in need, Kelly remained, for McGavin, the most appealing woman he'd ever known.

Faces appeared in the doorway of the lounge, drawn by the scuffle. There was much alarm and murmuring upon seeing the madam in handcuffs. Everyone scrambled. The doorway—the house— quickly emptied.

The young prostitute was beginning to calm down.

Kelly said, "Looks like murder's a good way to clear out a whorehouse."

McGavin guided Tran Le toward the lounge exit. She

was allowing herself to be led in sullen, brooding silence.

McGavin said, "I'll find a phone and call the MPs. Way this town is rigged, I call the Saigon cops or ARVN and Mr. Smith here will be back out on the street by tomorrow." He winked at his wife, for her eyes only. "I want this wrapped up ASAP, Miss Carpenter. Then it's back home."

"Glad to hear it," said Kelly and those green eyes of hers glinted greener than usual. "You and I have some unfinished business to take care of."

A Look At Dragonfire!
(Cody's War 1)

....

BIG TROUBLE IN CHINA!

Cody's mission: locate and extract a defecting phys-icist, Dr. Kwan, creator of the ghastly mega-weapon, Dragonfire. But the mission goes south almost immediate-ly when a US Navy reconnaissance plane disappears over the South China Sea after observing Chinese nuclear sub-marine activity. Also missing: the dive team sent to investi-gate. Then there's the coup d'état being staged in Beijing by renegade Chinese military officers intent on launching a nuclear holocaust and establishing a new World Order.

With no one to trust in this deadly maze, Jack Cody races the clock against an imminent world threat spawned far beneath the sea . . .

AVAILABLE NOW

About the Author

....

Stephen Mertz is an American fiction author who is best known for his mainstream thrillers and novels of suspense. His work covers a wide variety of styles from paranormal dark suspense to historical speculative) and hardboiled noir. Mertz is also a popular lecturer on the craft of writing and has appeared as a guest speaker before writer's groups and at universities. His work on Don Pendleton's Mack Bolan series is regarded by fans as some of the best in that series. He also created the Mark Stone: MIA Hunter and Cody's Army series, written under the pseudonyms Jack Buchanan and Jim Case respectively.

Stephen Mertz lives in the American Southwest, and he is always at work on a new book.